PRAISE FOR

KRISTINE KATHRYN RUSCH

"Rusch is a great storyteller."

—*RT Book Reviews*

"Whether [Rusch] writes high fantasy, horror, sf, or contemporary fantasy, I've always been fascinated by her ability to tell a story with that enviable gift of invisible prose. She's one of those very few writers whose style takes me right into the story—the words and pages disappear as the characters and their story swallows me whole….Rusch has style."

—Charles de Lint

"A masterful writer is at work."

—Orson Scott Card

"Rusch's greatest strength…is her ability to close down a story and leave the reader feeling that the author could not possibly have wrung any more satisfaction out of the piece."

—*The Kansas City Star*

"Rusch is a great storyteller—easily the equal of Patterson or Koontz."

—*Analog*

"Kristine Kathryn Rusch is one of the best writers in the field."

—*SFRevu*

"[Rusch's] writing style is simple but elegant, and her characterization excellent."

—Mark Morris
Beyond

"Kristine Kathryn Rusch's crime stories are exceptional, both in plot and in style."

—Ed Gorman
Mystery Scene Magazines

Praise for the Retrieval Artist series

"If you love puzzle mysteries, crime novels, well-invented sci-fi worlds, or stories about characters you can believe in and care about, you owe it to yourself to give Rusch's Retrieval Artist novels a try."

—Orson Scott Card
New York Times bestselling author

"What links [Miles Flint] to his most memorable literary ancestors is his hard-won ability to perceive the complex nature of morality and live with the burden of his own inevitable failure."

—*Locus*

Praise for the Diving series (novellas)

"Tense and gripping, the interpersonal conflicts kick this story up a notch. The endlessly enjoyable terror of dark, alien, empty spaces brimming with unknowable danger and impenetrable mystery should keep fans of the genre hooked."

—*The Internet Review of Science Fiction* on *Diving into the Wreck*

"The room of the title lurks at the heart of a mysterious space station built by an unknown intelligence; those unfortunate enough to venture into it disappear, die, or both. The station and the Room become an object of obsession and an almost religious devotion for those who search for the key to its mysteries. ... It's got a fascinating air of menace..."

—*SF Gospel* on *The Room of Lost Souls*

"This entry into the 'Diving' canon is a doozy ... a suspenseful story of a large spaceship returning to base, and finding that the base is quite different to normal."

—*Best SF* on *Becoming One With the Ghosts*

"'Becoming One With the Ghosts' is great stuff even if you've not read a previous story in this series, but if you have been following the series, Rusch adds wonderful depth to her world-building and universe."

—*SFRevu* on *Becoming One With the Ghosts*

Also by
Kristine Kathryn Rusch

The Retrieval Artist Series:

The Disappeared
Extremes
Consequences
Buried Deep
Paloma
Recovery Man
Duplicate Effort
Anniversary Day
Blowback

The Diving Series (novellas):

Diving into the Wreck
The Room of Lost Souls
Becalmed
Becoming One with the Ghosts
Stealth
Strangers at the Room of Lost Souls
The Spires of Denon

FIVE GOOFY
Science Fiction Stories

KRISTINE KATHRYN RUSCH

WMG PUBLISHING

Five Goofy Science Fiction Stories

Published 2013 by WMG Publishing
www.wmgpublishing.com

Cover design by Allyson Longueira/WMG Publishing
ISBN-13: 978-0-615-80976-2
ISBN-10: 0-615-80976-6

"Advisors at Naptime" by Kristine Kathryn Rusch first published in *If I Were An Evil Overlord*, edited by Martin H. Greenberg and Russell Davis, Daw Books, March 2007.

"The One That Got Away" by Kristine Kathryn Rusch first published in *The UFO Files*, edited by Martin H. Greenberg and Ed Gorman, Daw Books, 1998.

"Paparazzi of Dreams," by Kristine Kathryn Rusch first published in *Analog SF Magazine*, November, 2004.

"Going Native" by Kristine Kathryn Rusch first published in *Amazing Stories*, Fall, 1998.

"What Fluffy Knew," by Kristine Kathryn Rusch first published in *Alien Pets*, edited by Denise Little, Daw Books, 1998.

Contents

FIVE GOOFY
Science Fiction Stories

Introduction

I have a decidedly weird sense of humor. I have always seen the world in odd ways, but rarely did I speak of it because people looked at me strangely. They couldn't tell if I was serious or joking. And they weren't sure which they preferred—the serious me or the joking me.

It wasn't until I wrote my first romance novel, *Utterly Charming*, under the pen name Kristine Grayson that I felt free to admit I even had a sense of humor. For some reason, people think it funny that Prince Charming would fall in love with Sleeping Beauty's lawyer. It makes perfect sense to me.

Just like it makes perfect sense to me that a little girl who wants a nap would inadvertently save the world ("Advisors at Naptime") or that a cat who wants pampering would stop an alien invasion ("What Fluffy Knew"). Because I can't help myself, I occasionally lampoon my former profession, journalism, although the target is getting much too easy these days ("Going Native"). I like writing about casinos, but usually I write serious stories about them. It's tough to find anything serious about a blackjack tournament in a blackout, so I didn't even try ("The One That Got Away"). Of course, I may be serious about a topic like, say, copyright, but that doesn't stop me from having an off-beat perspective about it ("Paparazzi of Dreams").

If you asked me, I'd tell you that I only write funny romance stories with a touch of fantasy. But this collection proves that I lie. If you're looking for serious, award-winning fiction, look elsewhere. Here the strange prevails.

Enjoy.

—Kristine Kathryn Rusch
Lincoln City, Oregon
November 1, 2010

Advisors at Naptime

It was time for Carol's nap. They always forgot her nap. Mommy says every kid needs a nap. Carol used to hate naps, but now she's *tired*. All she wanted was her blankie, her cuddly dog, and her squishy pillow.

And Mommy. They never let Mommy into the playroom with her.

They said Mommy sat outside, but once they left the door unlocked and Carol got out. She was in a cold hallway that looked like a giant tube or something. No chairs, icky white lights, and a hard gray floor.

No Mommy, no guards, no one to hear if she cried.

She stamped her foot and screamed. Everybody came running. Mommy said they were watching a TV screen with Carol on it in that room up there—and then she pointed at this tiny window, way up at the end of the hall—and Carol got mad.

"You lied," she said, pointing her finger at Mommy in that way Mommy said was rude and mean. "You promised. You'd be right here. You said!"

Mommy got all flustered. Her cheeks got kinda pink when she was flustered and she messed with her hair, twirling it like she yelled at Carol for doing.

"I meant," Mommy said in that voice she gets when she's upset, "I'd be able to see you all the time."

"You said—"

"I know what I said, honey." Mommy looked at one of the guards—they're these big guys with square faces and these weird helmets you could see through. They also had big guns on their sides, latched down so nobody can grab them away—and then she looked back at Carol. "I meant I'd be able to see you. I'm sorry I said it wrong."

Carol wiped at her face. It was wet. She was crying and she didn't know it. She *hated* that. She hated this place. It wasn't fun like Mommy said it would be. It was a stinky place filled with grown-ups who didn't get it.

Mommy said she'd be playing games all day, and she did, kinda, but by herself. She sat in front of this computer and punched numbers.

Once this scary guy came in. He wore bright reds, and he kinda looked like a clown. He bent down like grown-ups do, and talked to her like she was really stupid.

He said, "Carol, my dear, I'm so glad you're going to help me with my little project. We'll have fun."

Only she never saw him again.

Which was good, because she didn't like him. He was fake cheery. She *hated* fake cheery. If he was gonna be icky, he should just be icky instead of pretending to be all happy and stuff. But she didn't tell him that. She didn't tell him a lot of stuff because she didn't like him. And she never saw him again. Just his mittens.

Mommy said every important person had mittens. Everybody who worked for him could be called a mitten, which meant Carol was one, even though she didn't look like a mitten. She finally figured it was some kinda code word—everybody here liked code words—for workers.

She thought it was a stupid one—Mommy would say, *be careful of Lord Kafir and his mittens*—and Carol would have to try not to laugh. How can people be afraid of big fake-cheery guys with mittens? 'Specially when they had big red shoes and shiny red pants like those clowns at that circus Uncle Reeve took her to.

Carol had a lot of uncles. Mommy used to bring them over a lot. Then she met Lord Kafir, and the uncles didn't come to the house no more. Lord Kafir promised Mommy a lot of money if Carol would play games at the Castle with him.

Mommy asked if this was a Neverland Ranch kinda thing and Lord Kafir's mittens—the ones who'd come to the house—looked surprised. Those mittens didn't wear helmets. They wore suits like real grown-ups and they had sunglasses and guns that Carol had seen on TV.

They wouldn't let her touch the guns (she *hated* it when grown-ups wouldn't let her touch stuff) but they promised she'd be playing with "weapons" all the time.

Mommy had to explain that weapons were like guns and stuff, only cooler.

So here's what Carol thought then: she thought she'd be going to a real castle, like that one they show on the

Disney Channel—maybe a blue one, maybe a pink one, with Tinkerbell flying around it, and lots of sparkly lights. She thought she'd get to wear a pretty dress like Cinderella, and dance with giant mice who were really nice, or meet a handsome beast like Belle did.

All the girls who go to castles get to wear pretty dresses with sparkly shoes, and they got to grow their hair really long (Mommy keeps Carol's hair short because "it's easier") and got to dance what Mommy called a walls, and they lived happily ever after.

But that's not what happened. The Castle wasn't a castle. It's this big building all gray and dark that's built into a mountain. The door let you in and said stuff like *checking, checking, all clear* before you got to go through another door.

Then there was the mittens. The ones outside the mountain door wore suits and sunglasses. The ones inside actually had the helmets and weird-looking guns and big boots. They scared Mommy—the mittens did, not the boots—and she almost left there. But the assistant, Miss Hanaday, joined them and talked to Mommy and reminded her about all the money she'd get for just three months of Carol's time (Carol didn't like that), and Mommy grabbed Carol's hand really tight and led her right into the castle/hall/mountain like it was okay.

Carol dug her feet in. She was wearing her prettiest shoes—all black and shiny (but no heels. Mommy says little girls can't wear heels)—and they scraped on that gray floor, leaving black marks. Mommy yelled at her, and Carol hunched even harder, because the place smelled bad, like doctors or that school she went to for three days, and Mommy said the smell was just air-conditioning, but they had air-conditioning at home and it didn't smell like this. At home, it smelled like the Jones's dog when he got wet. Here it smelled cold and metal and—wrong.

Carol hated it, but Mommy didn't care. She said, "Just three months," then took Carol to this room with all the stuff where she was supposed to play with Lord Kafir, and that's when Mommy said she'd be right outside.

So Mommy lied—and Carol hated liars.

And now all she wanted was a nap, and nobody was listening because Mommy was a liar and nobody was in that room. Carol was gonna scream and pound things if they didn't let her nap really soon. She wanted her blankie. She wanted her bed.

She wanted to be let out of this room.

She didn't care how many cookies they gave her for getting stuff right. She *hated* it here.

"Hate it," she said, pounding on the keyboard of the computer they had in here. "Hate it, hate it, hate it."

Each time she said "hate," her fist hit the keyboard. It jumped and made a squoogy sound. She kinda liked that sound. It was better than the stupid baby music they played in here or the dumb TV shows that she'd never seen before.

She wanted her movies. She wanted her big screen. She wanted her blankie and her bed.

She wanted a nap.

She pounded again, and Mommy opened the door.

"Honey, you're supposed to be looking at the pretty pictures."

She was leaning in and her cheeks was pink. If her hands wasn't grabbing the door, they'd be twirling her hair, and she might even be chewing on it.

"I don't like the pictures," Carol said.

"Honey—"

"I wanna go home."

"Tonight, honey."

"*Now*," Carol said.

"Honey, we're here to work for Lord Kafir."

"Don't like him." Carol crossed her arms.

"You're not supposed to like him."

"He's s'posed to play with me."

"No, honey, you're supposed to play with his toys."

"A computer's not a toy." Carol was just repeating what Mommy had told her over and over.

"No, dear, but the programs are. You're supposed to look at them and—"

"The bad guy always wins," Carol said. She *hated* it here. She wanted to see Simba or Belle or her friends on the TV. Or maybe go back to that kindergarten that Mommy hated because they said Carol was average. She didn't know what average was 'cept Mommy didn't like it. Mommy made it sound bad.

Until that day when she was looking at the want ads like she did (*Honey, don't mess with the paper. Mommy needs to read the want ads*) and then she looked up at Carol with that goofy frowny look and whispered, "Average five year old…"

"What?" Mommy asked.

"In the games," Carol said. "The bad guy always wins."

Mommy slid into the room and closed the door. "The bad guy's supposed to win, honey."

"No, he's not!" Carol shouted. "He gets blowed up or his parrot leaves him or the other lions eat him or he gets runned over by a big truck or his spaceship crashes. The good guys win."

Mommy shushed her and made up-and-down quiet motions with her hands. "Lord Kafir's a good guy."

"I'm not talkin 'bout him!" Carol was still shouting. Shouting felt good when you couldn't have a nap. "On the computer. The bad guys always win. It's a stupid game. I *hate* that game."

"Maybe you could do the numbers for a while, then, honey."

"The numbers, you hit the right button and they make stupid words. Nobody thinks I know letters but I do." Carol learned her ABCs a long time ago. "What's D-E-A-T-H-R-A-Y?"

"Candy," Mommy said. Her voice sounded funny.

Carol frowned. That didn't sound right.

"What's I-R-A-Q?"

Mommy grabbed her hair and twirled it. "Chocolate."

"What's W-H-I-T-E-H-O-U-S-E?" Carol asked.

"That's in there?" Mommy's face got all red.

"What's W-O-R-L-D-D-O-M-I-N-A-T-I-O-N?" Carol asked.

"D…D…O…" Mommy was frowning now too. "Oh. Oh!"

"See?" Carol said. "Stupid words. I hate stupid words and dumb numbers. And games where the bad guy wins. I want to go home, Mommy."

"Um, sure," Mommy said. She looked at the door, then at Carol. "Later. We'll go later."

"*Now*," Carol said.

Mommy shook her head. "Carol, honey, you know we can't leave until five."

"I wanna nap!" Carol shouted, then felt her own cheeks get hot. She never asked for a nap before. "And a cookie. And my cuddly dog and my pillow. I wanna go away. I hate it here, Mommy. I hate it."

"We have to keep coming, honey. We promised."

"No." Carol said and swung her chair around so she was looking at the computer.

It was blinking bright red. It never did that before.

"Mommy, look." Carol pointed at the big red word.

Mommy looked behind her like she thought somebody might come in the room. "Honey, I'm not supposed to see this—"

"What's that say?"

Mommy looked. Then Mommy grabbed Carol real tight, and ran for the door. She got it open, but all those mittens with guns and helmets was outside, with guns pointed.

Mommy stopped. "Please let us go. Please."

"I'm sorry, Ma'am," the man with the biggest gun said. "You have to wait for Ms. Hanaday."

"We can't wait for Ms. Hanaday," Mommy said. "My daughter punched the computer. Now it's counting down to a self-destruct."

Carol squirmed. She watched *Star Trek*. She knew what a self-destruct was. "We gots to go," she whispered.

Mommy just squeezed her tighter.

"We gots to go!" Carol shouted.

Mommy nodded.

The guards kept their guns on them.

"A self-destruct?" one of them whispered.

Another guard elbowed him. "She's the average five-year-old. She finds the holes before we implement the program."

"Huh?" the first guard asked.

"Y'know, how they always say that the plan's so bad an average five-year-old could figure out how to get around it? She's the average—"

"Enough!" Mommy said. "I don't care if it is fake. I'm not going to take that risk."

Carol squirmed. She wanted to kick, but Mommy hated it when she kicked. Sometimes Carol got in trouble for kicking Mommy. Not always. Sometimes Mommy forgot to yell at her. But right now, Mommy was stressed. She'd yell.

"I'm sorry, ma'am," the first guard said. "We can't let you go until Ms. Hanaday gets here."

"And she is!" a lady's voice said from far away. Carol peered around Mommy, and sure enough, there was that Ms. Hanaday, in her high heels and her black suit and wearing her glasses halfway down her nose even though she wasn't as old as Mommy was.

"I wanna go," Carol whispered.

"I know, honey," Mommy said, but she wasn't listening. She was just talking like she did when Carol was bugging her. But she did set Carol down, only she kept a hold of Carol's hand so Carol couldn't run away.

Ms. Hanaday was holding a bag. Her heels made clicky noises on the hard gray floor. It was colder out here than it was in that room. Carol shivered. She wanted a jacket. She wanted her blankie. She wanted a nap.

"I wanna go home," she said again.

One of the guards looked at her real nice-like. He was somebody's daddy, she just knew it. Maybe if she acted just a little cuter...

"What have we got here?" Ms. Hanaday said as she got close. She reached into the bag, and crouched at the same time. She whipped out a giant chocolate chip cookie, the kind Mommy said had to last at least three meals.

Carol reached for it, but Mommy grabbed her hand.

"We would like to leave now," Mommy said.

"May I remind you, Ms. Rogers, that you signed a three-month contract? It's only been three weeks."

"Still. My daughter isn't happy, and I'm not real comfortable here. No child should have to work all day."

"It's not designed as work, ma'am. It's play."

"Is not," Carol muttered, wanting that cookie. She stared at it. Maybe if she stared hard enough, it would float over to her. She seen that in movies too.

"Did you hear her?" Mommy asked. "She doesn't think it's play."

"Wanna nap," Carol told Ms. Hanaday.

Really want that cookie, but Mommy still had a hold of her hand. Too tight. Mommy's hand was cold and kinda sweaty.

Ms. Hanaday was frowning at her.

"I don't like it here," Carol said louder this time, in case Ms. Hanady didn't hear so good. "Wanna go."

"The day's not over yet," Ms. Hanaday said.

"Delores!" Lord Kafir shouted from down the hall. Carol knew it was him because he had the funny accent Mommy called Brid Ish. Some people from England had it. Most of them got to be bad guys in movies.

Carol shivered again.

Ms. Hanaday stood up. Lord Kafir was hurrying down the hall. His shoes didn't make that clicky sound. They were kinda quiet, maybe because they weren't official grownup shoes.

"Is it true?" he asked Ms. Hanaday like there wasn't Mommy and Carol and all those guys with the big guns. "Did she break the code?"

"I'm afraid so," Ms. Hanaday said. She was holding the cookie so hard part of it broke. She had to move really fast to catch it before it fell to the ground.

Now the cookie was Carol-size. Carol looked at Mommy, but Mommy wasn't looking at her.

"This is the five-year-old, right?" Lord Kafir pushed past Ms. Hanaday, knocking the cookie again. She had to grab real fast and still parts of it fell on the floor. Wasted. Carol wanted to get them, but Mommy wouldn't let her go.

"Yes, sir. This is Carol. You've met her."

"That's right." He crouched.

Carol made a face at him. She hated people who forgot her.

"You look pretty smart," he said.

"I'm tired," she said.

"Are you smart?" he asked.

"Of course I am, dummy," Carol said.

"Carol!" Mommy breathed. "We don't talk to grown-ups like that."

He wasn't a grown-up. He was a mean man in bright red clothes. He was glaring at her like she'd done something wrong.

"I think you're pretty smart," he said like that was bad.

"Her teachers said she was average," Mommy said.

"We tested her IQ three times. She always came out in the normal range." Ms. Hanaday sounded kinda scared.

"You know that children often give unreliable IQ tests." Lord Kafir pushed up and looked at the other grown-ups. "I don't think she's average."

"Mr.—Lord—Sir," Mommy said. "She's—"

"The other five-year-olds couldn't beat that self-destruct," he said.

"They barely got a chance, sir." Ms. Hanaday was dripping cookie crumbs. "She got it earlier than the others—"

"Because she solved the earlier puzzles sooner. She's good at code words and passwords and secret plans. She shouldn't be this good if she's average."

"She watches a lot of television," Mommy said.

"Can I have that cookie?" Carol asked.

Everybody looked at her.

"Please?" she asked in her best company voice.

"Oh, for heaven's sake," Mommy said, but Ms. Hanaday handed her all the parts of the cookie.

Carol chomped. The cookie wasn't as good as it looked. Maybe because it got all sweaty and gooey in Ms. Hanaday's hand.

"I swear, sir," Ms. Hanaday said. "She's average."

"I'm tired of five-year-olds," he said. "It's time to implement the plan."

"Sir! We can't do that! It's not ready!" Ms. Hanaday said.

"Get it ready," he said.

"But the five-year-old—"

"Isn't average," he said.

Ms. Hanaday looked at Mommy like Mommy had gone into the living room without permission. It was like that code grown-ups had. Lord Kafir understood, even if Carol didn't.

"Have you seen anything?" Lord Kafir asked Mommy.

"No," Mommy said. She was lying. Carol looked at her in shock. Mommy was a horrible liar. She lied all the time. Carol just didn't know it before.

"She saw the red lights," Carol said. She didn't want Mommy to get in trouble with Lord Kafir. "It scared her."

"Red scares a lot of people," he said, smoothing his ugly clothes. Was that why he wore them? To scare people?

The guards looked at each other, like they didn't like any of this.

Ms. Hanaday shook her head.

"Pay the lady her three weeks and get them out of here," Lord Kafir said to her. "And wash your hands. You're a mess."

"Yes, sir," Ms. Hanaday said, but Lord Kafir was already hurrying down the hall.

The guards had lowered their weapons.

Ms. Hanaday ran a hand through her hair, making a streak of chocolate on the side of her face. It looked a little like poo.

Carol tried not to giggle.

"You know that this is all just war games," Ms. Hanaday said.

"Sure," Mommy said.

"Pretend stuff," Ms. Hanaday said.

"Yeah," Mommy said.

"None of it means anything," Ms. Hanaday said.

"I know," Mommy said.

"I'll get your check," Ms. Hanaday said, "and meet you at the door."

"Okay," Mommy said.

Ms. Hanaday hurried off after Lord Kafir. The guards just stared after her.

"I don't like this," one said to the other.

Mommy picked Carol up like she was a baby. "We're going, honey."

Carol swallowed the last of the cookie. Cookies were yucky without milk. "Okay," she said.

Mommy hurried down the hall, a different way than everybody else went. It only took a few minutes to get to the door.

Ms. Hanaday was already there, holding a long piece of paper. It had to be a check. Mommy snatched it, then said thanks in a kinda rude voice, and then hurried out the door.

Nobody stopped them. In the movies, somebody would've stopped them. 'Specially the way Mommy was breathing, like she was all scared and stuff.

Carol wasn't scared. Carol was glad to be outside where the sun was bright and the air smelled really good. She stretched. She wanted down. She wanted to run, but Mommy held tight all the way to the car.

They backed up and headed out of the parking lot, driving really, really fast.

"If you want a nap," Mommy said, "close your eyes."

"Where're we going?" Carol asked.

"Far away," Mommy said.

"Can we get my blankie?"

"Maybe," Mommy said. That meant no. Carol sighed. She hated no. But not as much as she hated that place.

"What's far away?" Carol asked.

"Good guys," Mommy said.

Carol smiled. This was how it was supposed to go. She leaned back in her chair and closed her eyes. But she couldn't sleep. Mommy was driving really bad. Fast like in the movies. Tires squealing. Going around corners on two wheels, stuff like that.

Mommy'd been watching Carol play too many games.

Carol opened her eyes. They were on a road outta town. Carol'd never been outta town before. This was kinda cool.

"Mommy?"

"Hmm?" Mommy said in that don't-bother-me voice.

"Am I average?"

"I hope so, honey," Mommy said. "In fact, I'm praying that you are."

"Because average kids beat the game?" Carol asked.

"And that means it's easy," Mommy said.

It didn't seem easy. It was just dumb. But Carol didn't say that. She closed her eyes again. She didn't care about numbers and weird letters and computers. Or bad guys like Lord Kafir. They could be scary, but they always lost in the end.

At least she got part of what she wanted. She got a cookie. She got outta there.

And now—*finally*—she was gonna take a nap.

The One That Got Away

It happened at the Thursday night blackjack tournament, and we were miffed. Not because it happened, but because of *when* it happened. And to get to that will take a bit of explaining, both about the tournament and about us.

There are about ten of us, and we call ourselves the Tuesday/Thursday regulars because we never miss a tournament. The local Native American casino—the Spirit Winds—held an open tournament every Tuesday and Thursday. Anyone could play if he put up twenty bucks, and if he won, he got a share of the pot. The pot consisted of the buy-in fees, and the buy-back fees plus another hundred added by the casino. The casino made no money on the tournament. The game was a freebie designed to get people into the casino—and it got me there twice a week.

Me, and nine others. There were more regulars than us, of course, but we were the ones who never skipped a week. I was a pretty good player—I'd made a living counting cards in the mid-seventies—and I'd swear that Tigo Jones had professional card-playing experience as well. Five more of the regulars played basic strategy, and the rest, well, they relied upon luck or God or their moods to supply their strategy. It worked for them every once in a while.

In blackjack, you learn to honor luck.

The good players just try to minimize it. They try to rely on skill. But luck can win out, in the end, if you're not careful.

On most nights, pot's only worth about two hundred to the winner, a hundred to second place, and fifty to third, with four dinner comps to sop the folks who made it to the final round. What that means is that there's good money in this for me and Tigo because we place every four tournaments we play. A few regulars are losing money each time they play, and about five—those basic strategy guys—are giving their gambling fund an occasional shot in the arm.

It's all in good fun, and we've become a family of sorts—the kind of family that barflies make or old ladies make when they work on church social after church social. We look after each other, and we gossip about each other, and we tolerate each other, whether we like each other or not.

We also know who's crazy and who isn't, and, except for Joey, the kid who is pissing his inheritance away twenty dollars at a time, no one who shows up for the blackjack tournaments at Spirit Winds is crazy.

Or, at least, that's what we hope.

***

That night, I noticed a few strange things before I even made it to Spirit Winds. For one thing, the ocean was so black it was impossible to see. Now, the ocean is never black. It reflects light—and even if the sky is completely dark, the ocean isn't because it's reflecting the light of nearby homes. In fact, I like the ocean on cloudy nights because it has a luminescence all its own, a glow that makes it look alive from within.

The second strange thing was that there was no wind. None. Zero, zip, zilch. We usually have a breeze in Seavy Village and often have more than that. The ocean again. It is a major part of our lives.

And the final strange thing was the power outage that swept through the neighborhoods like anxious fingers pinching out candles. I didn't know about that until later—the casino has back up generators—and if I had known, well, it would have made no difference.

I would have been at the tournament anyway.

I have nothing better to do.

You see, I call myself retired, but really what I am is hiding out. I'm good enough to play in big tournaments, but when Spirit Winds holds its semi-annual $10,000 tournament, I'm conveniently out of town. That way, I don't have to fill out a 1099, and I don't have to show three pieces of i.d, and all the correct tax information. Because I don't have three valid pieces of i.d, and I haven't filed taxes since 1978, the year I fled Nevada with the wrong kind of folks at my heels. I moved too fast to get any fake i.d., and so I lived off cash for far too long. By the time I had settled down, I didn't know anybody in that business any more. The government had closed the loopholes making fake ids simple for anyone with half a brain, and I really didn't want to put fingers out to the criminal element, since it was the criminal element I'd been running from.

I confessed to a local banker with hippie sympathies, let him think I had been underground since my college activist days, and had him set me up a checking account. It's amazing what a man can do with a checking account—the lies he can tell to get him a real life in a small town.

But it couldn't get me a driver's license, nor could it get me a credit card. I still use cash much of the time, and a lot of that cash comes from my safety deposit box in the aforementioned bank. The gambling at the small casino is just incidental. I figure I'm old enough now that no one would recognize me and my problem is so out of date that the folks who were looking for me are either dead or in prison. But I have learned to be cautious by nature. I don't rub anyone the wrong way.

And I never, ever call attention to myself.

***

The tournament was big that night, bigger than it had ever been. Later I learned the reason: the power outage. The casino was packed on a Thursday because much of Seavy Village had lost their lights, their heat, and their cable. I had been in the casino since mid-afternoon. I'd been on a roll at one of the regular tables, parlaying my lucky hundred dollar chip into six thousand. Normally that puts you in tax declaration territory, but I would get five hundred on one table, then pocket it, and move to the next. I was hot that afternoon, and it felt good.

Lucky streaks are important. Knowing how to maximize them is even more important, and that's what I was doing. Perfecting the old skills.

When I reached six grand, my brain shut off, and I decided to replenish it with food. I had a solitary dinner at the buffet, and then wandered to the tournament tables.

There were a lot of unfamiliar faces around the table, and I was burdened with a small fortune in chips, stuck in my pockets and my fanny pack. I couldn't take anything to the car because I didn't have one, and I also didn't have time to walk home. I'd been in that situation before, and I'd learned not to be too friendly. The last time I'd told one of the regulars about my run and a pit boss overheard. I had to spend a good fifteen minutes making a show of losing the money at various tables.

Normally the pit bosses don't tell on me. They tolerate me and Tigo and the other local professionals. It's the out-of-towners they kick out of the casino. Oregonians and their dislike of "foreigners." Gotta love 'em.

That night, though, I wasn't taking any chances. I leaned against one of the slot machines and smoked a cigarette, adding to the thick, slightly bluish air already growing around the tables. The casino is new and modern,—no tokens for slots, only cash and cards—high ceilings, good traffic flow. The place feels more like a spa than a casino, especially the casinos of my heyday. I still miss the chink-chink of tokens as they clink out of the machines. I'm not sure I'll ever get used to those electronic beeps. But not even the modern recycling system was taking care of the cigarette smoke. In a blue-collar town like Seavy Village, card players get nervous when more than $50 is on the line.

That night, forty players had signed up for the tournament, and the pot tipped a grand for the first time since the casino opened.

***

I'll leave out the detailed descriptions of the rounds, although I can recite all of it, every card, every bet, from the first round, the semi-final round, and the buy-back round. I know by what percentage Tigo beat the odds when he doubled down on eighteen and got a three. I know the exact moment luck abandoned Cherise, and it wasn't when she drew a twenty to the dealer's twenty-one. I even know that I made a small mistake on the twenty-ninth hand, and if the cards hadn't gone my way, I would have been out—deservedly so—and it would have peeved me to no end.

I rarely make mistakes.

I can't afford it.

No. I won't say much about the game except that tempers flared early, even among the regulars, because of the amount of money on the table. And people left angry when they were eliminated because everyone could taste their share of the pot.

When it came to the final hand, only the players and the regulars were left.

Tigo and I were on the table, of course, along with the idiot Joey whose luck was running better than usual, and Smoky Butler who was a dealer at another casino on the other side of the coast range. The rest of the players weren't regulars. Two were bad betters and even worse strategists who managed to get the right cards at the right time, and the other one was a black-haired woman who'd caught all of our attention.

She looked like she should be in Monte Carlo, not Seavy Village, Oregon. She wore a black cocktail dress cut in a modified v that revealed more cleavage than I had seen in years. Her hair was pulled into a chignon and over it she wore a cloche hat complete with small veil. Her lips were dark red, and she smoked a cigarette through a cigarette holder.

And she wasn't lucky.

She was good.

Almost as good as me.

The cards were running hot and cold that night, and our pal Joey's luck ran out first. He was off the table in five hands. Then we lost the first of the two bad betters. The second was holding in, but not worth our time. He was out by the eleventh hand.

The rest of us, though. The rest of us had a game.

For our buy-in, the casino gives us $500 in tournament chips (which you can't carry to the real tables) per game. The winner, of course, is the person with the most chips after fifteen hands.

By end of the eleventh hand, I had fifteen hundred eighty-five dollars in phony chips.

Tigo had fifteen hundred seventy-five.

Smoky Butler had fifteen hundred and fifty.

And the woman, well, she had two thousand even.

For the first time since I'd left Nevada, I was in a blackjack game where everyone knew how to play. That meant they knew how to draw cards, they knew how to bet, and they knew strategy.

I damned near licked my lips and rubbed my hands together in glee. Instead, I crouched over my chips as if I were protecting them from prying eyes.

We all put out our bets.

The lady put out a hundred.

Smoky put out a hundred and fifty.

Tigo a hundred and twenty-five.

And me, a hundred and fifteen.

Then Rosco, the dealer, began the hand. I was first base (a revolving position), and he gave me an ace of clubs.

Followed by an ace of diamonds for Tigo, an ace of spades for Smoky, and an ace of hearts for the lady.

"They should be playing poker," someone said from behind me.

Rosco gave himself a three of hearts. Then he reached toward the shoe for my next card.

At that moment, the lights went out. The place was pitch black except for several small red dots made by the tips of a hundred cigarettes. I fell across my cards and chips, and Rosco yelled, "Freeze!" to the tournament players. The pit bosses were yelling and the dealers were shouting orders, and some old lady near the slots was wailing at the top of her lungs.

All the time, I kept thinking that this shouldn't be happening. It couldn't be happening. The casino had generators. They should have kicked in. (At the time, I didn't know they'd already kicked in, which meant that they shouldn't have gone off—at least, not all at once.)

Then the lights came back up, or I thought they did, until I realized that the overhead lights in the casino were white, not green. Everyone looked as if they were peering at each other through a fish tank. Even the mystery lady looked green. She was holding her cigarette holder over her chips, and glaring at us all angrily, as if we had caused the problem.

The pit bosses were looking mighty scared. I don't know how much money they had to protect, in chips mostly because the cash disappeared into slots beneath the tables, but I knew it was a lot. And there were more civilians in the casino than pit bosses. Security guards had stationed themselves near the casino banks, and other employees had fanned themselves around the room.

I had never seen anything like it, but it made sense. The casino had to have a drill policy for all types of emergencies.

The place was hot and smoky and everything was green. I kept my hands over my chips and scanned for the source of the light.

As I did, a wind came up. First it licked my hair—or what's left of it—and then it cleared the smoke. At first, I thought the air recycling system had turned back on. Then I realized something greater was happening here.

The source of the green lights were small dervishes the size of my coffee saucers at home. They looked like the alien spaceship out of *E.T.*, only shrunk down into toy specials for MacDonalds' Happy Meals. Except they worked. Their top was a dark cone, and their base was a rotating series of lights, all various shades of green.

And there must have been thousands of them in that small space. Maybe even millions of them.

They hovered over various tables, avoided the slot machines, and disappeared into the back. The poker room was filled with them. I could see them from my vantage points, lined up like tiny aircraft carriers facing a city, the poker players backing against the wall, hands up.

Five crafts found their places over our table, and a sixth placed itself above the dealer. The woman pulled a small pistol from her handbag, and a pit boss immediately grabbed it from her—firearms are illegal on Indian land. He pointed it, wobbling for a moment, at one of the little crafts, then Rosco said, "If you shoot one and it explodes and we get that green goo all over us and we die, you're going to regret that."

"He'll regret it more if the bullet hits one of us," Smoky said.

"It could ricochet," Tigo added.

The pit boss let the weapon fall to his side. The woman glared at him.

"I wouldn't have missed," she said, as if she blamed him for taking away her opportunity.

The little crafts were above us, whirling and creating the breeze. Rosco had his hand on the money slot. So, it seemed, did every other dealer in the place. We all stared at the things.

"What are they?" Tigo whispered.

I took the question as rhetorical, and apparently everyone else did too because no one answered him.

One of the pit bosses was on the phone, talking with the 911 dispatch. He was whispering loudly, so loudly he may as well have been shouting: "No, really, I'm not kidding. Please..."

Aside from the whirs, the soft mumbles of scared patrons, and the wailing woman, the casino was eerily quiet. No electronic beeps and buzzes, no blaring music, no tinkling chords of winning slots. The silence unnerved me more than anything.

"What do they want?" Tigo whispered.

"Ask them," Smoky snapped.

"I feel like I'm in a James Bond movie," the woman said, and that started a ripple of panic through the pit bosses. They apparently hadn't thought of the things as high tech theft devices.

"If you were in a James Bond movie, my dear," I said, "you'd have better lighting." No one looked good in that ugly green. Not even the most beautiful woman in the place.

Then, as if on cue, green lights flared out of the bottom of the tiny crafts. I backed away from the table, chips forgotten. So did everyone else. Rosco let go of his hold on the money slot, and one of the pit bosses screamed at him but—I noted—did not make a move toward the money, the table or any of the lights.

The lights hit the table and I expected to see big burning holes appear. I was ready to run for cover—all of this going through my mind in the half second it took, mind you—when I realized what was going on.

The cards rose off the surface, whirling and twirling as if they were in a tornado. For a moment, the entire casino was filled with swirling cards. It looked like an elaborate fan dance, or as if green sea gulls were swarming the beach or like an electronic kaleidoscope performance designed especially for us.

Then one by one the cards slid into the crafts through a slot in the sides. They made a slight ca-thunk! as they entered. Then the green tractor lights—what else could they be called?—went out, and the little green ships whirled away.

The doormen and the folks in the parking lot at the time all say the little ships sped out the doors and into a larger ship that had been hovering over the ocean. A number of green slots opened on it, letting the little ships through, and then they disappeared into the night.

The ocean, which had been dark, regained its luminescence, and slowly the lights flickered on all over town.

At least, that's what the outdoor folks said.

Inside, it was chaos. People started shouting and screaming, and that wailing woman continued. A few people stampeded toward the door, and one relatively fit young man got trampled just enough to later attempt a suit against the casino.

Then the lights came back on. The slot machines groaned as they started up, then beeped through their start-up protocol. The slot players, the video poker players, and the keno players all continued with their games except for a few sensible folks who decided to call it a night and left.

I have no idea what happened inside the poker room, but at the tournament table, we counted our chips. The pit bosses put the game on hold as they made sure the money was fine.

It soon became clear the only thing missing from the casino were the cards.

All of them.

Including the decks stored in the back rooms, and the discards waiting to be trucked off the place, and even the little souvenir cards in the gift shop.

Gone.

All gone.

The pit boss who had called 911 was off the phone, saying the police were going to arrive soon, but I suspected it would take them some time. If, as people were saying, things were a mess all over town, it would take the police a while to get anywhere.

"We still have money on the table," Smoky said.

"And a game to finish," Tigo said.

"How do you propose we do that with no cards?" Rosco asked.

"We know what was dealt," the woman said

"But we don't know the order in the rest of the shoe," I said.

"We're going to shuffle a new shoe and start over," Rosco said, "just as soon as we get cards."

"We need the other three players," Tigo said. I glanced around me. Joe was standing behind me as he usually did after he got knocked out of a tournament, but the others were nowhere to be seen.

"We're going to have to put this game on hold until the cops arrive anyway," the pit boss said.

"Until we get cards," Rosco added.

"Besides, everyone'll have to report what they saw," Smoky said.

At that point, the woman and I both stood up. "I think my luck has just run out," the woman said.

"Mine, too," I said.

We left the table and headed toward the door.

"Hey!" Tigo said behind us. "We can't replay the game without you guys!"

"I think the game is forfeit," the woman said.

"Yeah, have the casino put the pot in for next week," I said, knowing they never would.

Then she and I walked through the casino, side by side. The conversations were strangely muted, only a few people discussing what they saw. As we stepped outside, we ran into chaos, cars cramming the parking lot, attendants staring at the sky, a warm bath of light all over the town.

A familiar bath of light.

I had missed it more than I realized.

I turned to her. "There's a nice coffee place about a block from here. Care for a walk?"

"I'd love it," she said.

And we had a nice cup of coffee, and a nice evening, and a nice night, and an even better morning. I never learned her name and she never learned mine, but we both knew that we had left the casino for the exact same reason.

We didn't need to see the police.

Or the media.

Or anyone else, for that matter.

"What do you think they wanted with the cards?" she asked long around midnight.

"I don't know," I said. "Maybe they use bigger shoes than we do."

And a little later, I said, "That, by far, has to be the strangest thing I ever saw in a casino."

"Really?" she responded. "I've seen stranger."

But she never elaborated and I didn't ask her to.

Some stories are better kept close to the vest.

You see, that isn't the strangest thing I'd ever seen in a casino either.

But it's the only one I'll admit to.

And I only do that because I'm a regular and it's a shared group experience. A bit of local legend—the one game that never finished, the pot that got away.

Well away. The casino had to shut down both the poker and blackjack tables for two days while it ordered cards from all over the country. During that time, regulars gave interviews on every show from *CNN* to *Inside Edition*. Except for me.

I laid low for a while even after my lady left. Laid low and watched the skies.

And wondered—

What would have happened on the thirteenth hand if we had all blackjacked on the twelfth?

What would have happened then?

Paparazzi of Dreams

"I don't get it," she says, adjusting the telephoto.

It's all about waiting—her and me, sitting in the car, waiting for the sun to go down, waiting for our third—Ryan—to signal that Xavier has gone to bed. I'm stuck in the passenger seat with Morgana to my left. She's the experienced one; I'm the rookie. At least, that's how I'm playing it.

We're parked at the end of a dirt road just outside the gate. The guard hasn't seen us, won't come down even if he does. Just call the sheriff and we're off, gone before anyone gets here because we not only have a scanner, we have headquarters with their moles in the various law enforcement agencies all over the country monitoring every call.

Celebrityville USA. We're all so lucky that everyone wants a piece of the action.

"I mean," Morgana says, still fiddling with the focus. She's using the damn camera as a spyglass. "My dreams are just as crazed. Really. The last time I got Xavier, we get the standard naked-in-front-of a crowd thing. And you know, it's from his point of view, so except for that quick take at his johnson, we don't see much of anything—just crowd reaction and laughter, lots of laughter. Hell, I can have that dream on my own."

Not with a johnson, I think, but of course I don't say that. I keep my own counsel. Hell, I even keep my own name. I am undercover with the Dream Merchants. They all call me Max, and I've been here long enough to answer to it.

I bite my fingernail so that I don't give Morgana my first answer. The first answer would've been the honest one: if you think this is all such a crock, why the hell do you do it?

But I know why she does it. I've seen the money. I watch the kids buying this stuff, readily packaged by the mass-market conglomerates, the ones that used to sponsor magazines and stuff on glitz. Smart corporate execs—they figured out, once the dream technology became viable, that other people's dreams sold well on the Internet. Digitized, compartmentalized, surreal as hell.

The car is cold. Night on the beach, tiny towns. Celebs should know better than to trust locals with information about travel. Northern California was once the celeb hotspot, then they all had to move north. Oregon kept its secrets for the longest time—poorest state in the nation by the teens, lots of hunger, lots of need for work—desperate people don't talk much.

But in the last few years, the economy has turned around and word is getting out. Nur and Catherine with their palace on the Elbow; Sappho (stupid name, that) and Jenella in Yachats; and of course, Xavier—once Xavier and

Lorita—with their very famous house just outside of Depoe Bay.

Lorita moved on to Cannes—what goes around comes around, they say, and what was hot will be again—but Xavier stayed after the divorce. Word is that she got the career, and he got the money, but for all her Oscars, he's still ranked number one at the box office.

And because of that, his dreams are worth almost as much as his pictures. More, if you count the price per second. Only he doesn't get automatic ownership. The dream has to be in a permanent form before that happens: recorded, copyrighted, registered.

That's where I come in.

Or at least, where I'm supposed to come in. My motorbike is parked inside the back of the van. We get the recording, I head to the nearest node, and I download the entire thing, along with the proper documentation, to the copyright office.

A few more of these, and I'll be trusted enough that no one'll double-check me. I'll be able to move up in the company, maybe even go into the private offices, view the records, see if anyone is breaking any real laws.

We try to shut these places down one by one, but it's hard. Mostly I'm gathering evidence for a creative artists' lobbying group, one that wants Congress to change the copyright laws to account for the changes in technology. My bosses want to make dream theft illegal: my job is to find ways to convince the politicians that it's worthwhile to buck the multi-billion dollar entertainment industry.

Morgana finally sets the camera down. She pushes the dispenser button on the coffeemaker in the dash. She fills her mug, then points to it. "You look like you need some."

I do, but I hate the generic crap she uses. In my car, which is currently residing in Jersey until I'm done with this stupid assignment, I have primo European beans, roasted to perfection and ground the moment I press dispense. Then boiling water shoots through the grounds, a shot of powdered milk (still can't keep the real stuff—there are limits to technology, even now), and a touch of sugar, and I have the perfect cup.

I miss it.

"You don't even seem thrilled that we're gonna get Xavier," Morgana says.

Oops. Mistake on my part. Rookies should always be slavering for the big celeb get.

"Xavier's been got before. You said so yourself just a few minutes ago."

"Yeah, but there's always the possibility we'll get the max dream, you know? The one that replays the split memories with him and Lorita, or maybe the one that mixes his real memories with some fantasy he's having."

"Everyone has dreams like that," I say.

"But not based in life. When you dream about Lorita, Max, you dream about the woman you've seen on the screen. When Xavier dreams of her, you know you're getting the woman he's seen and touched and tasted."

"Too bad dreams don't come in all five senses," I say.

Morgana blows on the mug, trying to cool the brew. It stinks of oil and cheap water. The beans smell old. "They're working it. They say within ten years, we'll be able to have it all—smells, touch, taste—everything."

Except that running commentary we sometimes get when we dream: that dialogue about the future or about your worries or about the way it actually feels to stand naked in front of a crowd.

Last time I had that dream, complete with my johnson looking as tired as it does in life, I was standing in front of sixteen refreshers at the detective agency that hires me out, trying to explain the intricacies of copyright law as it pertains to our clients.

I'm yammering about the differences between ownership of form versus the actual dream, and hoping that the class will understand how the law is always behind the technology, when I realize I'm cold. Not just any cold. Icebox cold. I look down—the famous johnson shot every man has in these dreams—and I don't think of covering it up.

Instead, I get someone to close a window. And then I go on. The class doesn't look; the class doesn't laugh. They're all taking notes, and as I call up the information they're typing on their PDAs, I see that the class is actually taking notes on what I say, not on what I look like.

And, I have to admit, there was a sense of disappointment I can still feel. A sense of disappointment that, if some paparazzi were stealing my dream through a telephoto attached to one of those special cameras, wouldn't come through. Some parts of dreams are still private—even now.

"Lights out." Ryan's voice sounds small and oddly rich through the digitized intercom on Morgana's busy dash.

Morgana hits the timer she glued to the edge of the steering wheel. The damn timer makes an actual ticking sound, like those antique clocks rich people like to keep in their living rooms.

I slip on my leather gloves, my heart starting to pound. The next fifteen minutes are crucial: Ryan can't get caught; he has to get the dream—there has to be a dream—and then he has to get back to us, before I can head off on the bike.

At least we're doing Xavier tonight. Pretty Xavier Calliende, so famous he's only known by one name. All of America—hell, all of the world—recognizes that five-five frame, that boyish face with its fashionable golden skin and smoky eyes. He's been dream-captured so much that even his sleep habits are well known. It only takes him five minutes from lights out to REM—hence Morgana's timer—and his dreams tend to rotate through pretty fast.

We only have time to wait through the first REM cycle: Much longer than that, and we're as close to getting caught as possible. Someday, Morgana wants to find a way to arrive and set up in the middle of the night: rumor has it that Xavier's best dreams happen before dawn, but the guards shift at that time, so there are twice as many people on the estate, making it nearly impossible to collect the pre-dawn REM.

The ticking continues. I slip on my bomber jacket, and adjust the collar so that the automatic helmet doesn't hit me in the neck when I activate the damn thing. Precisely ten minutes into the wait, I'll head to the bike—provided we get some kind of communication from Ryan.

Then I just wait—again—until he comes crashing through the bushes with his little prize.

Five minutes in, Morgana relaxes like she's the one dreaming. She sips the last of her crap coffee, then dispenses another cup, not offering me one this time. I won't have time to drink it if all goes to plan.

The oil-and-old-bean smell makes my stomach turn. Stakeouts were bad enough when I was a rookie detective on homicide. Then I quit, and joined a major D.C. detective agency, thinking that job might be more interesting.

It wasn't: mostly political stake-outs, trying to catch some politician in a controversial act. I jumped at the chance to work for the lobbying group.

They taught me that what companies like the Dream Merchants do isn't really illegal—not yet, anyway. The dreams are—to use the words of the damn techs—floating out there for anyone to pick up. Freedom of expression belongs to the person who codifies it, kinda like shouts heard at a rally.

Of course celebs control how their images are used, but here's the beauty of dream marketing: most of us don't see ourselves in our dreams. We're the protagonist, the point-of-view character, and there's no "image" involved.

It's all in the process of change, of course. Celebs are picketing Congress, and one or two of the senators have had their dreams stolen, so they know what a violation of privacy it really is.

The timer dings softly. Ten minutes.

Morgana looks at me, tilts her head slightly, her regal command to get my butt out of the car and on the way to the cycle.

"We don't know if he has something yet," I say, mostly because I hate these coastal nights, with their fog and damp chill and instant cold. It's July, for crissakes, and it's fifty-five degrees out there, if I'm lucky.

"Just get ready," she says. "I'll signal you."

I roll my eyes, ease the car door open, and wince as the fog seeps into the interior. I gotta ride in this stuff. I'll be happy when we move operations back to the City of Angels, where nights are seventy-five and balmy and I don't have to worry about sliding off some cliff in the foggy dark.

As I climb out, I hear Ryan's voice, all rich and velvety in the intercom. "Long REM. But I think I got the bulk. I'm seeing extra guards, so I'm heading out."

I push the door closed, careful not to let the latch make a telltale click. There aren't any guards near this part of the gate, but you can't be too careful. The last thing I want is to get caught—trespassing is still illegal, and we're within breathing range of that silly little crime.

I slink along the side of the car, crouching so that my head isn't visible above the roof. Dream Merchants know what they're doing; their vehicles are all camouflage-equipped. When the camo isn't on, this one is a dusky gray. But right now, the exterior is sliding from green to black, depending on the light.

My bike also has camo, and I almost can't see it along the car's back edge. But I feel for the handlebars, find them, and flick the dismount switch.

The level lowers the bike to the ground—the hydraulics almost silent in the evening air. In fact, aside from a few confused birds and ever-present shush-shush of the Pacific, I'm not catching much of anything. Even the highway is quiet, something that's mighty rare on 101 in the summer.

Then I hear it: the crunch of leaves, the heavy breathing, the snap of branches as they move back and forth. I climb on the bike's leather seat, touch the collar of my bomber jacket and duck as the automatic helmet curls out of the jacket's back and form-fits around my head.

I slide my fingers over the automatic controls, rev up the silent engine (which has always struck me as a contradiction in terms) and wait—yet again—holding my breath.

Through the glazed window, I see Morgana giving me a thumbs up, telling me what I already know. The great crashing sounds, the sobbing breaths, the creature looming through the forest that Xavier bought is Ryan, with the handful of guards coming right after him.

Ryan scales the fence like a monkey, the camera around his neck. He's skinny and barely twenty, and more athletic than he should be, given his diet of cappuccinos and pizza. He flips over the fence, and somehow manages to land on his feet, catlike.

He slides up next to me, hands me three discs—the important one no bigger than my thumb; the other two decoys in case the guards catch me—and hurries to the passenger side of the car.

I spin the bike out, heading down the gravel driveway as fast as I can. My wheels spit gravel and I long for a bigger windshield, but those, as my Dream Merchants bike trainer insisted, are for wimps. I hunch down, my head barely above the bars, and let the bike skid and slide its way to the highway.

The guards know where I'm going. Even though we're almost three decades into the new century, there's still only one artery on the Oregon Coastline, and that's Highway 101. The question is whether I'll go south or north.

If I were banking on me, and of course I'm not, I'd head north to Lincoln City and all the tech stuff that migrated over here fifteen years ago.

Instead, I hit 101 for all of five blocks, then cross the bridge in the center of Depoe Bay, heading toward the Coast Guard station, down in the World's Smallest Harbor. There's a government node there, one most people don't know about, and I'm gambling Xavier's guards fall into the most people category.

Soon as I reach the Coast Guard station, I'm off the bike, the helmet's gone, and the bike is stashed behind a Jeep Wrangler that has probably seen half a million miles. My bomber jacket is gone and I'm freezing my ass off, but I'm walking like a local—the sleeves of my sweatshirt pushed up, my thumbs hooked in the pockets of my jeans like this is any old night.

I get to the node, punch in the all-express number for the Copyright Office, add Dream Merchants' privacy code, and download the raw REM from Xavier, along with the date and my employee code.

Xavier, still warm in his bed, probably dreaming of Lorita like half of America, doesn't realize that the dreams he probably can't even remember—the starter dreams that his brain first cycled out just after midnight—are now the property of Dream Merchants.

And, if those dreams are any good, they'll be uploaded before Xavier begins his rumored main dream cycle at dawn.

***

The team picks me up in front of the Sea Hag, the oldest restaurant in this tiny burg. I walked up from the Coast Guard station. Morgana drives back down, louvers the bike onto the back of the car, and we head to the condo Dream Merchants is paying for just north of the city.

The views are spectacular, even in the middle of the night. The ocean has a kind of glow, some of which is reflected light from nearby hotels. The rest comes from the stars—the real ones—and the moon and the ocean's general ambience, all white foam and violent water.

It's way too back to nature for me.

I'm the last one into the condo, after spending a few minutes on the balcony, watching the guards drive aimlessly back and forth searching for a green-black car or a single-rider motorcycle. One sheriff's vehicle got added to the search but didn't do much. Some wag on the police scanner opined that we were halfway to Portland by now—showing no one completely understood the operation, which Morgana took to be a good thing.

Soon the whole search will be called off. Law enforcement can't do much—they haven't witnessed the so-called trespassing, after all—and the guards do have a duty to Xavier: they can't leave his place vulnerable all night.

By the time I go inside, Morgana has the gas fireplace on high, the windows shaded and the radio beside the door on so loud you'd think she hasn't yet reached her sixteenth birthday.

She and Ryan are huddled in what passes for the living room—a high-ceilinged narrow room with floor-to-ceiling windows and the hardest sofa I've ever had the misfortune to sit in. Fortunately, Ryan's hogging it, so I have to bring one of the kitchen chairs into the room.

Morgana's tweaking the download, trying to get high rez enhancement, going for vivid colors—a hallmark of Xavier dreams, as opposed to dreams posing as Xavier dreams. In addition to being one of the biggest stars in the world, Xavier's one of those minority of people who dream in colors so vivid Jackson Pollack would have been jealous—if he were alive, dreaming, and trying to make a fortune off the uncensored images in his head.

"Mostly fragments," Morgana says, spitting the words, as if it's Ryan's fault that Xavier's most recent dreams had no logical consistency. Fragments can be sold as individual images, but they don't command the prices that the full-story dreams do.

A few vendors arrange the fragments like they are a dream, but the fans catch onto that trick pretty quickly, and often avoid repeat visits to those sites. So Morgana's under strict orders to find linked images first and foremost.

Ryan puts his hands behind his head and stretches out on that uncomfortable couch. He watches the get, unconcerned by Morgana's tone.

"Finally," she says, as the images bump and settle into something passing for an actual dream.

I lean forward, interested in spite of myself.

Xavier's dream starts mundanely enough: Our Point of View Character—obviously Xavier himself—is sitting on an embankment in the middle of a filthy downtown. Takes me a minute to realize we're in Chicago about twenty years ago, before Xavier is Xavier, and before I'm even old enough to vote.

Xavier's wearing torn blue jeans and scuffed Nikes, and they don't look like the uniform of the day. They look like the best he's got. He's breathing hard, sifting embankment dirt through his grimy fingers like he's looking for something or waiting for someone and needs something to do with his hands.

Then the image focuses on those hands and what I take for grime is actually blood. Above him, an L train clankety-clanks by, and the embankment is gone. We're down in the Loop in the days before the L got upgraded to bullet train, back when the tracks were rusted and made of a thick metal that came from the middle of the previous century.

Xavier's got a girl pressed up against the staircase, and they seem to be alone. She's begging him, and I realize after a second that she's not begging him to touch her like most women would nowadays, she's begging him to let her go. Her breath is pretty raspy and her eyes are awful big, glassy—not with drugs or lack of sleep, but actual pain.

Then I recognize his grunts, and know what he's doing and a tear squeezes out of her left eye as she turns her face away.

The moment after he finishes, he zips up—the sound almost the only thing in that surreal scene—then she shoves him, hard, so that he stumbles backwards.

But he recovers, pushing her back, and she slams into the wrought iron steps. He grabs her, shoves her again, and again, until her head doesn't look female any more. Blood's spattering, more blood than would ever be at that kind of crime scene. The streets just run with it. He slaps her again and suddenly Morgana's fast-forwarding.

"What the hell're you doing?" I ask before I realize that I probably shouldn't speak.

"Seeing if there's anything good here," she says.

"That's not classic," I say. "It's not the long-empty-hallway dream or the falling dream or your basic wet dream. It's—"

"A goddamn rerun," Morgana says. "He has this thing damn near once a week, and it's fucking useless. Ice

Cream Dreams has owned this thing for ten years, and it's practically the same frame for frame. It's one of his repeaters, and it isn't even very popular. It's just somewhere that his brain stutters to with too much regularity, and not enough variation to make it worthwhile for the rest of us."

The dream ends with the rivers of blood flowing into Lake Michigan. This image goes on for what seems like forever, or maybe it only does because Morgana is fast-forwarding. Hell, when Xavier dreams it, there might be some overlying commentary or music or maybe even screaming from the dead girl, but for the rest of us, watching an unenhanced dream, all we get is blood and silence.

Morgana slows the fast-forward down when we reach Xavier again, sitting on an embankment. Only this time, he's not beside the L. He's sitting on a tree-lined shore that leads into the blood-filled lake.

In the distance, little sailboats dot the horizon, white against the blue sky, a nice ironic counterpoint to the red water, and the blood on Xavier's hands.

I'm shaking. Ryan is asleep. Morgana is cursing under her breath. She sits even closer to the screen, studying it for some kind of difference and apparently not finding any.

The REM section ends with a few more fragments—floating faces, a bit of blood, a woman screaming as her eyes grow wide—and then it all ends.

Morgana freeze-frames the last image—the screaming woman—and curses again.

"A wasted night. I should be doing still photography for all the good this is doing me." She runs a hand through her hair and then snaps the screen off. "Fuck. You paid a fee on the copyright, didn't you, Max?"

"Following instructions," I say as laconically as I can manage. My heart is still racing from those dream images. He has that dream more than once a week? Has anyone tripped to the significance of that?

Morgana sighs. "At least it's unfiltered REM. We won't get in trouble for poaching on Ice Cream Dreams' material."

"It's the form," I say idly, and then wish I hadn't.

Morgana swivels, focuses on me as if I'm the REM recording. "What?"

I'm supposed to be a rookie, someone who knows nothing. But I might have just blown that image. I try to recover as best I can by pretending I don't know that I said something I shouldn't even understand.

"That's what you're always harping on," I say. "The perfect form. That's the problem with the other dream factories, you say. They don't know how to make their forms work even when the dream-story is lame. So I figure the copyright office shouldn't care, right? It's just the form that's the problem, and we sent an unfiltered capture. It's bound to be different than the unfiltered capture sent by Ice Cream Dreams however long ago. And it's definitely different from the one they eventually started to sell."

Her gaze is sharp, measuring. She glances briefly at Ryan, but he snuffles, asleep, not even famous enough for either of us to grab his camera and record his dreams.

"You're learning awful fast," she says.

I shrug.

"I don't think I've ever had an assistant who learned this fast." That measuring gaze would've made me uncomfortable if I hadn't spent so many years as a cop, perfecting a gaze like that myself. Still, I'm not sure how to play it—as someone who does feel uneasy under a heavy stare, or as someone who doesn't.

After a moment, I say, "You make that sound like a bad thing."

Now it's Morgana's turn to shrug. "I can't figure you out, Max. You're not excited by the get. You find snuff dreams fascinating, and you understand form. You sure you didn't do this before? Maybe some illegal stuff? Porn? Underage vids? Teen wet dreams?"

I feel my shoulders relax. She's going the wrong direction with this. She thinks I've got more experience in the business than I let on, not that I'm undercover.

"No," I say. "But I don't think this is rocket science."

She laughs, picks up the equipment, and pops the get out of the machine.

"Still," I say, "that dream is fascinating."

"Worthless." She picks up the equipment. "He's going to be in this burg for a few more days, but I'm not sure I want to waste any more time on him. Maybe Xavier's passé."

"Maybe for you," I say, "but have you considered what the dream means?"

"Oh, don't get all creepy weird on me, Max. I like you. I thought you were level-headed." She stuffs the get into a nearby bag, then shoves the screen against the wall. She gets on the love seat, and stares at the fake fire, ignoring the very real ocean which is visible in the window next to her.

"I am level-headed," I say. "I thought you were too."

She frowns at me, then glances at Ryan. He snorts again, deep in some REM sleep of his own.

"What are you getting at?" she asks.

"You said it a minute ago," I say. "You make money off celebs. That's your job, right? A kind of paparazzi of dreams."

"Hell, I used to be the real thing," she says, like being any kind of paparazzi at all is a respectable job.

"And if you're like me, you contract with Dream Merchants on a per-job basis because it's not worth their while to have anyone on staff, particularly if the gets fade or go a different way."

She's watching me now as closely as she had a few moments ago, but this time her dark eyes are avid. She's hearing money talk, which appeals to her.

"So?" she says.

"So, I assume you've studied dream theory?"

"It's crap," she says. "Who cares if flying is a sex dream or going through a damn tunnel is a metaphor for the penis entering the vagina?"

"That's not what I'm talking about," I say. "That *is* crap. I'm talking about the real stuff, the stuff they've figured out that's like real science."

She crosses her arms. "What? That everyone dreams? That you don't live long if you don't dream? That images change from culture-to-culture, but remain the same if you were brought up in the same tradition? Yeah, I got all that and it's worth about as much as the air I just used to tell you about it."

"You missed one," I say.

She sighs. Morgana likes to play games, but hates it when other people do. "What?"

"Repeated dreams," I say.

"Stress- or guilt-related, or maybe building on some other kind of emotion." Her voice is flat like she's reciting from a textbook. "Happens when the dreamer is feeling that emotion and the brain believes that emotion needs to be relieved, which is why most of these things are stress dreams. However, Xavier's main stress dream is one where he walks into a studio for a big movie, and they tell him they gave the part to some two-bit newcomer, and he can just leave. Or, the variation is that he is already acting in the role, asking everyone if he's good enough, and finally, they tell him no, he's not, and then the two-bit newcomer takes his place."

"I'm not talking about Xavier or stress dreams," I say, which isn't entirely true. I am talking about Xavier, and maybe I should shut up. Maybe I should just let this one go. It's my old cop instincts, the ones that gave me my own personal stress dream—walking up to a crime scene, seeing the perp pull the crime off, and trying to stop him, only to find myself wrapped in plastic, unable to move. "I'm talking about memories."

"Fuck." Morgana leans back in her chair. "You had me going for a minute there."

"Huh?"

"You can't prove someone else's dream is a memory," she says.

"Sure you can," I say, "and they've done it, repeatedly, particularly with famous folks. Since a lot of these people became famous due to a single—often traumatic—event."

Maybe this is cop work. Maybe I am giving myself away. But there's a part of me that really doesn't care. This work is impersonal and it does burn you out. Or maybe I'm just a bit disgusted at my own reaction to the dream, that hint of excitement I felt, as if I really did understand the get and the high it gives.

"You're talking about survivors of accidents and stuff?" Morgana asks.

I have her attention now.

"Movie-of-the-week kinda people?" she asks.

"Yeah," I say.

"I don't work that low," she says. "I don't think I've even thought of getting a get from the fifteen-minutes-of-fame folks."

It's my turn to sigh. She's more familiar with Xavier than I am, and I'm intrigued enough to need information. Only I have to go at it as if I'm not, as if we're two people sitting in a car, waiting for someone else to record the dreams of yet another person.

"I don't care how low you work," I say, because in my book, it's pretty low even now. "I'm talking about a studied phenomenon. They've realized with those people that they'll relive the trauma in their dreams over and over and over again. Usually detail for detail."

"Like a repeat." Her plucked brows come together. She bites her lower lip, obviously thinking.

"You say Xavier has that dream every week?" I lean forward on my chair, brace my elbows on my knees, and look at her.

She doesn't move—at least not much. If nothing else, her eyes get narrower. "Yeah."

"So maybe it's more than a repeat. Maybe it's a memory."

"Of a film role?" she asks.

"Maybe," I say. "I don't watch his movies. I wouldn't know a damn thing about him if he weren't a get."

"Started modeling, hired off the street back about eighteen years ago, when some talent agency was looking for 'the real thing,' not some generic pretty boy. Gets an agent and a manager, makes some real money, they find him bit parts, the camera loves him, and he has one of those break-through teen idol movies—"

"*Heartbeat*," I say, because I do know something about him, and because that movie was impossible to avoid. Just like the post-*Heartbeat* publicity when he falls in love with his leading lady, Lorita, who had already had two Hollywood marriages behind her, and this one—she says at the time—is the one that's gonna last.

Of course it doesn't. But by then, Xavier's on the map, and he's got some kind of golden touch, something that makes him choose the movies that connect with a generation. You name the best movies of the last ten years, and Xavier's been in most of them.

"*Heartbeat*," Morgana says, shaking her head. "The damn thing still holds up."

As if it's a century old instead of a decade. But, I suppose, if you live day-to-day, the way she does, a decade does feel like a hundred years.

"Hell," she says, "if you don't know what happened after that, then what in God's name are you doing in this job?"

"I know what happened," I say. "I just haven't seen any of his films."

Partial lie. I don't remember the ones I have seen. I catch them late-night, and realize about halfway through that I have watched the damn thing before, and it's such fluff that it made no impression at all.

"Consequently," I say, "I don't know if those dream images we just watched are from some movie."

Morgana raises her eyebrows. "Our Hero Xavier raping and murdering a girl? He didn't even do that in *Double Double* where he plays both the protag and the villain."

"Not even the early stuff?" I ask.

"Maybe the modeling," she says. "But I had to go back through the shoots once, and I don't remember anything violent. They used him for the clean stuff, you know, aftershave and clothing and cars. Nothing that would appeal to the rougher crowd."

And as she says this last, her voice slows down. She's figuring it out.

My heart is pounding, and my breathing's a little ragged, and that makes me uncomfortable. I'm not sure I like how I'm thinking, so I ignore it.

Ryan, thank God, is still snoring on the couch.

"You think this might have actually happened?" Morgana asks, finally. "You think Xavier might have raped and murdered some girl?"

"Two points to the lady," I say.

"Shit." She stands up, unable to sit with the idea. She paces to the screen, then grabs Ryan's souped-up camera, staring at it, thinking about the images it stole out of thin air. I'm staring at it too, wondering why I'm so hyped, and basically knowing even though I don't want to.

The cop's get: solving an unsolved. But I'm not a cop any more, and I'm not interested in that get. I'm working government and business now, protecting creativity and creative minds all over the country.

Yeah, right.

"Shit," she says again. "That's like combining the old and the new."

"Huh?"

She threw me with that one. I don't know what she's talking about. Then she crooks her finger at me, leads me out of the condo's living room away from snoring Ryan.

We go into the first bedroom, then beyond, into the square box that passes for a kitchen. She grabs a Diet Coke out of the fridge and sits at the table, opens a window so that we get ocean noise, and taps her fingernails on the can.

"Old and new," she says, "the ultimate get. You know, the dreams that aren't dreams but memories. The memories that expose a celeb in a way that's sensationalistic, breaking an exposé that'll be everyone else's get for a week, maybe even months. It's got everything, Max."

Okay, so she is ahead of me.

"Everything?" I ask.

"You gotta know the history of celebrity. It's full of crimes of the century, trials of the century, ruined careers, and tabloids, tabloids, tabloids. Then we get TV, and tabloid shows. Then the Internet comes along, and the tabloids become hourly, you know, the get of the gets. The dreams, they're just a high-paying version of the photograph—the chopper over the wedding stuff—but they don't pay the way a sensational get does, particularly if you're the one who breaks it and controls the information."

Her face is flushed. I've never seen her so thrilled.

"You don't just control the flow, eventually you become part of the story. Book deals, movies of your own—"

"And you become one of those fifteen-minutes-of-famers," I say, trying to keep myself calm.

"If you're bad at it, sure," she says. "Or it's the get of a lifetime, and you make a career out of it, you become the expert on dream memories or subconscious crimes or whatever. You become the go-to person. See, that's part of the history of celebrity, too. The Louella Parsons, and Walter Winchell, and Barbara Walters and the goddamn tears, and *Entertainment Tonight* and Sanford Cooper and all those folks. They started with a major get, and they parlayed that get into a career of gets."

"The second-tier celebrity," I say, using another of her terms.

"Shit, no," she says. "The celebrity journalist. A lot of these folks—Hedda Hopper, Liz Smith—they're not just chasing the get, they *create* it. In her day, Hopper was the one who used her influence to create the celebrities or destroy them."

"Power," I whisper.

And Morgana smiles. "Now you're getting it, Max."

"All from one possible murder," I say.

"A celeb murder pre-fame," she says, "that no one's nailed down."

"And yet," I say, "it might only be a dream."

"Or a scene from a movie," she says.

"Or one of his fantasies," I say.

"Yuck," she says, as if her life and imagination are pure. She guzzles the Diet Coke. "You know, I got some money stashed, and I'm getting mighty tired of sitting in cars, waiting for some lamo famous person's subconscious to vomit a storyline. Maybe we should chase these images."

"We?" I say, even though that was what I was initially going for. I thought I needed Morgana, but maybe not. I was going for the white-knight thing, solving a twenty-year old crime, but she's already made it something bigger—and something that intrigues me, against my better judgment.

"We, smart boy," she says. "You're the one who figured this out, so I assume you're the one who's done the reading on dreams and memory and crap. Besides, you like getting your hands dirty, all the background stuff. You told me that when I hired you and I remember thinking, 'Why the hell should I care?' Well, I care now, and it'll be really cool."

She turns things on me faster than I can imagine. I've never known anyone who controls the people around her like Morgana does. Usually I'm the one in charge, but in this case, it's her.

"What'll be cool?" I ask.

"The way we'll work together," Morgana says. "I'll head back to L.A. and dig up every image I can find of Xavier—even his goddamn baby pictures. You head off to—Where is that? D.C.?—and see if you can find the girl or what happened to her."

"It's Chicago," I say, wondering how she can miss the L or the lake. But places aren't Morgana's strong suit. People are.

"Fine," she says, "whatever. Blow into the Windy City and see if you can find this thing."

"Then what?" I ask.

"Then we break the get. We have the scoop of the century—or at least the decade. And it'll be news not just because Mr. I-Can't-Make-An-Unpopular-Movie murdered his way to stardom, but also because we used new technology to catch him."

She grins at me, and I feel even more off-balance. I was sort-of thinking along those lines—the arresting of a movie star lines—when I started talking to her, but not about individual and personal fame. That's Morgana's thing, not mine.

"What if I can't find anything?" I ask.

She shrugs. "Hell, we just spent a fortune on a get that turned out to be a repeat. I figure if you're gone for a frickin' month, burning 10K a day in expenses, the losses won't be any greater than this one was."

I would never spend 10K a day, but I don't tell her that. If she's willing to use the expense account to send me to Chicago and keep me out of the waiting/motorcycle gig, I'm a happy man.

"That's what I got?" I say. "A month?"

"Babe, you got half a year if you bring in the get." She grins at me. I've never seen Morgana so pleased. She reaches across the table and cups my face with her hand. Her skin is cold from the Coke can. "You're something else."

"Yeah," I say, wondering what I've just gotten myself into. "I certainly am."

***

The nice thing about undercover is you don't have to report in weekly, even monthly. The rough thing about it is that when you're done, you have to justify each action, explain your reasons for doing each and every little thing.

I lie awake in my narrow bed in the smallest room of the condo, listening to the surf pound and the occasional truck go by on 101, wondering if I should resign from the agency. Because this really has nothing to do with stealing dreams and putting them into a form. If I'm right about the get (and I cringe, realizing Morgana's language has seeped into my brain), then this is about an actual old-fashioned crime—murder—not a new-fangled, hard-to-prove, maybe-not-ever a crime, like dream theft.

Morgana's already out of here, heading to Portland to catch the six a.m. back to L.A. My flight's two days from now, giving me time to close up the condo and explain to Ryan why he'll be working with a new team. Ryan'll be just as happy as the rest of us to blow this burg—celebs like tiny towns for the intimacy and illusion of privacy, but these places are hell on the rest of us.

I can hardly wait to get to the Windy City and use my real training—digging through old records, opening a cold case, seeing if a real-life murder actually happened some twenty years ago in the Loop.

***

I spend the next night in Portland at Powell's City of Books, the biggest bookstore in the U.S. for going on thirty years now, buying every single volume I can find on Xavier and his cronies. There are way too many of these things, and I'm not happy looking like some overage fan boy with too much time on his hands. I even buy a black City of Books book bag just so that I don't have to carry these things around in public.

Ryan's still in Depoe Bay, still in the condo, waiting for the new team. He says he wants to get the ultimate Xavier get—which, in Ryan's mind, is still that predawn dream—and he's willing to sit on that fence in the cold damp air every night for the rest of his life to achieve it.

The new team'll answer to him. He seems relieved that Morgana's gone, and he's never really even noticed me. He'll forget that we were even there two days from now.

Me, by the time I get on the plane to Chi-Town, I know more than I ever wanted to know about the publicist's version of Xavier Calliende's childhood, youth, and pre-fame days.

It seems like there's a template for actors, at least the successful ones: broken homes, a lot of siblings, need for attention, poor school behavior rescued by love of the theater, a gift for performance or comedy or music. Xavier had all three according to his early teachers, and then he fell in with the wrong crowd. He was living on the streets when his pretty face got him a modeling job—kind of the 21st century version of getting discovered in a soda shop.

My cop self, reading between the lines, thinks no one noticed this kid until he suddenly ended up on the silver screen. The teachers hear his background, vaguely remember his face, look up their old class lists, and claim they remember him. He's tossed out of the house, heading down the drugs-and-alcohol path toward total ruin, most likely paying for his habits by turning tricks when one of those tricks actually looks at his face and realizes that this boy is a meal ticket.

I log on at thirty thousand feet, surf through the garbage on Xavier to the scandal sheets, figuring the tabloids that Morgana admires so much probably have the uncensored versions of Xavier's past—at least the stuff they dare publish without getting threats from Xavier's "people."

I find a lot of facts to confirm my guesses, along with some early names. I also search the old news wire databases for unsolved teen murders in Chicago, but get so many hits that I feel discouraged even before I start.

I log off, catch a few zzzs, startle awake when I realize that if I dream, anyone on the plane can peer into my brain. Not that I'm famous enough. Not that I'm interesting enough.

But this job has gotten to me, and that's when I realize how badly I need this break.

***

Chicago is an old-fashioned blue-collar town. Carl Sandburg called it the City with Big Shoulders, and not much has changed in the 100-plus years since he wrote that line. The people are blunt and hard-edged. They also come in all shapes and sizes, mostly a little overweight and a little underdressed.

Chicago reminds me how much I hate the world of celeb. All surface and glitter, all appearances and images—even the goddamn dreams. It's refreshing to hear someone curse me for grabbing a cab before they can; it's thrilling to have the clerk at the hotel treat me like I'm important rather than some nobody who's in town to view the stars; it's exhilarating to walk the streets and not scan passing people to see if they're someone I "know."

Once I'm inside my hotel room in one of the glitzy places on the north side of the river where, apparently, the money's always stayed since someone decided to settle in this swampland and call it a city. I am using the Dream Merchants expense account to live in comfort for the week—or months—that I'll be in the Second City, but I'm only using that account at the hotel.

The rest of the time Max has left the building. The rest of my time in Chicago will be as myself, Burton Kleeland, the former New York City policeman, here on assignment for my new job, working a cold case, tracking the background of a suspected criminal for a crime that happened decades ago. There won't be any mention of Xavier, or Dream Merchants or Hollywood. Only one dead girl, possibly raped and murdered, and left by the L for someone else to find.

It's amazing how easy it is to slip back into my old self. First thing I do is get rid of the Hollywood clothes—no jeans and ponytails and casual white shirt that somehow has to stay white. I clean off the fake tattoos and take out the earrings, glad I didn't get anything else pierced so that I looked like the middle-aged former metal-head I was supposed to be.

The secondhand stores in the Loop carried the rumpled clothes I needed to reclaim old Burt Kleeland. Jeans still—guys my age always wear jeans—but a suit jacket over them, an old suit jacket that has seen better days. A trench coat for the rain, and a shabby umbrella (same purpose). Button-down shirts for under the suit coat, and a few ties so that it looks like I'm trying to be serious about my job. I even get real shoes—the kind that have leather exteriors and look like they belonged to my father. I only plan to wear those when I have to flash my old badge at someone. The rest of the time I'm holding onto my Nikes.

Research in Chicago's a pleasant thing. This is a city that holds onto its history with big meaty fists. First, I go to the Chicago Cultural Center, a Romanesque building that had been built in the 1890s as the Chicago Public Library. The place smells cool and dry, probably a combination of the marble interior and the stone exterior, along with some sort of sophisticated air-conditioning system.

The Museum of Broadcasting lives in this place and while I like all the ancient television shows and the monuments to entertainers I've only seen on documentaries, I'm not in the mood to browse. What I want is the research center two floors up, manned by a disgruntled teenager and an elderly maven who spend their days handing out old-fashioned headphones for the old-fashioned equipment, and taking people's driver's licenses for the folks who want to work on the new equipment.

Me, I'm going for both. I want to see what Chicago thinks of its native son, Xavier Calliende. I want to see if the city's broadcast media recorded his meteoric rise to fame or jumped on the bandwagon afterwards.

And I want to use the scanning equipment for a few visual comparisons. They might cut some time off my work.

The cool quiet of the research library calms me quicker than a glass of wine. I haven't been in cool quiet for nearly a year. I've been alone with my own thoughts—all that damn waiting—but never looking at something that interests me, trying to figure out the past in the best way possible.

First I use the digital index to see what's in the archives about Xavier. I find the expected stuff—more recorded versions of *Entertainment Tonight* than anyone should be allowed to see; a few *Dateline: Entertainments;* and a lot of little movie-promotional feeds. Of course there's a *Biography* and all of the *Biography* rip-offs, as well as ancient, downloaded and perfectly preserved internet sites—as Morgana would say, little tiny pictures of a not-quite-real past.

I skip all of that. I'm looking for the local stuff, the stuff that often doesn't make it into the national consciousness. I want the Xavier only Chicago knows.

But after two hours of searching, it seems that the Xavier Chicago knows is the same one whom the rest of the world knows. My hunch about his past becomes even more real to me—Xavier was a nobody until somebody discovered him.

So I go back to the desk, hand them my driver's license and a fifty, and get the keycard for the image-comparison scanner. I also have to sign a waiver that I won't use this machine for nefarious purposes, and I must acknowledge that the Department of Homeland Security could be watching me at any time, worrying about the images I'm trying to compare. I could be a terrorist, after all—the bogeyman from my childhood.

I take the keycard and the little ID Number the disgruntled teenager gave me and wander into the secondary research room. This one's smaller than the main one, partly because the equipment's smaller. The old stuff is big and bulky, desktop sized. The new stuff fits in the palm of my hand.

I have to sit out in the open to do my work, unlike the other sections of the research library. The equipment is so small that I might steal it if the old biddy and the boy aren't watching my every move. (I'm sure they're not, but illusions are always more powerful than reality, even in research libraries.)

I take the freeze-framed dream image of the girl, her face half-turned away from the Protagonist's, a tear on her cheek, and plug it into the comparison scanner. It'll take a few minutes because I don't have a full-frame face.

I looked, of course. In fact, I searched for one. But even when Xavier's humping the girl, he's not really looking at her. Her face isn't quite there. It's almost like he couldn't quite remember her, and his brain wasn't willing to supply a new face in place of the old one.

The weird thing is, though, that the image of the tear-streaked half-turned face is so clear it's of photographic quality. If I were back on the old job, I could've used that face for a partial holographic 3-D reconstruct, and one of the forensic art and sculpt team could've used that partial to recreate the whole face.

I'd go to the Chicago Police Department and beg for help from their forensic unit if I have to, but until I do, I'm going to see what I can do on my own.

The little scanner in front of me beeps, then a printer next to me spits out two 8.5 x 11 single-spaced sheets of references with images that match this girl's face.

I grab the sheets as they emerge, my heart pounding. All the references are twenty years ago, just like we thought. But half of them are for a missing persons report. A quarter are news broadcasts from the same period. And the last quarter are a series of documentaries on the grisly and violent Loop Rapist—a man they caught literally red-handed.

***

Of course, I don't believe what I'm finding. Did Xavier pay off someone to take the fall for him? Was an innocent man accused? And worse, is Xavier Calliende, America's Favorite Action Hero, really the Loop Rapist?

A shiver runs through me that has nothing to do with the chilled recycled air.

I take my list and go back to the digitized index, checking out all of the news reports and two of the most reputable companies' documentaries. I also hang onto my keycard, just in case my scan is flawed.

But when I settle myself in the main room, in cubicles that were designed back in the late 1990s, and I plug my headphone into a jack that had been designed in the same period, I look at the image the biddy in the back has sent to my screen (patrons aren't allowed to touch the old videos and DVDs. We must give a reference number to the biddy, and then she puts everything into the machines. We poor peon patrons only get to watch.)

The image on my screen is high-quality reproduction of a missing poster, clearly designed by a loving family. A girl—what passed for an All-American Girl in my childhood—rounded cheeks, blue eyes, brownish blond hair and a fresh-faced smile—dominates the page. In one photograph, she's laughing and cuddling the All-American Dog—some kind of mid-sized mutt. In another, she's staring sideways at me, her hair done up, the background all foamy and pretty—a graduation photo.

And in the photo that matches Xavier's dream/memory vision, her face is turned sideways in the exact angle of the vision. She's looking at a friend who has been cut out of the photograph, and there are no tears on her cheeks. Her smile is soft and radiant, the kind of smile that girls get when they're in love.

I peer at the person the poster designers cut off: from what I can tell, it's not Xavier. All I have to go on is an arm, a shoulder, and a bit of hair. Hair changes color, but shoulders and arms have a certain sense of definition, and unless Xavier was really small and scrawny when he knew this girl, he isn't the guy in the photograph.

Then I look at the rest of the poster. It was clearly family-designed for an unexpectedly missing person. The girl's name was Holly Lescoe, and she was an honor student at one of the suburban high schools. She'd gone downtown to see a play with a friend, and neither girl had returned.

The story, apparently, was major local news because of the Loop Rapist, and because Holly was the All-American Girl. If an innocent like Holly, beautiful and smart (her whiteness implied), could become a victim of the Loop Rapist, anyone could.

And sure enough, a few weeks later, the community's worst fears had come true. Holly Lescoe, All-American Girl, had washed up on the shores of Lake Michigan. She'd been beaten so badly that it took dental records to identify her, and after the autopsy, the medical examiner confirmed rape.

I watch the coverage, read through the files. The only thing that ties the victims of the Loop Rapist together was that they were in the Loop and they were female. Otherwise, they have nothing in common—not ethnicity, not age, not occupation or attitude. They vary from teenage girls to elderly women, and they all died brutally: raped, beaten, and tossed into the lake.

One afternoon, about a year after Holly Lescoe's body washed up, an off-duty police officer sees a man carrying a bundle toward the boat docks near Jackson Park. The man scurries past when he notices the cop watching him.

The cop follows him, notes that the bundle is dripping red, and gets close enough to realize that the man is covered in blood. That's when the off-duty cop calls for back-up which miraculously arrives within five minutes, and they catch this guy, this Tony Knickerson, trying to dump a body into a boat. The boat's his, and the bottom is covered in guts and blood.

The guts belong to fish. The blood is human.

The physical evidence links Knickerson to all of the Loop Rapist killings. His semen is inside the bodies, his skin cells beneath several fingernails (apparently not washed away by that wily lake). Their blood is in his boat and on his clothes—since he never once tried to cover his tracks.

Tony Knickerson didn't even have a trial. He confessed as soon as he got inside and, in exchange for staying off death row, told the cops where to find more bodies. He went to prison for life.

I sit back in my chair, study all of the news footage before me—the girl whose face clearly belongs to Xavier's memory—and go over what I know.

I know that physical evidence of that magnitude is hard to fake. I also know that Xavier lived on the streets in those years. Literally on the streets, doing drugs and/or dealing them, possibly turning tricks. He probably saw lots of stuff he didn't want to see, lots of stuff he needed to forget.

Like the murder of Holly Lescoe?

That could as easily be a guilt dream as a memory dream. They are related, after all, and it would make some sense: he hadn't stepped in. He hadn't stopped the crime. He had seen it all, and he blamed himself.

I bite my lower lip as I consider: he saw her well enough to remember her face, remember the tears, but not well enough to see what she looked like during the rape. Had there been a period of time between? Had he tried to save her and failed?

Is Xavier Calliende's hero complex that simple? Is he a hero in his imagination and a failure in his life? Does he have to act that out on screen?

I don't know, and I'm not sure I care. I'm going to follow through on all of this, but it has lost its luster for me.

Even if I can prove that Xavier saw the crime, I can't charge him with anything. All we have is a dream, after all. No clear evidence that he could have stopped the killer. No clear evidence that Xavier hadn't made Holly Lescoe cry on his own, so that when he heard of her death, he was able to put the pieces together.

Actors have vivid imaginations—that's part of the job.

It's a dead end, a blind alley, and all of those other tacky clichés. Still, it got me away from Dream Merchants for a short time—a much needed break so that I can go back undercover and try to get enough evidence to convince Congress to create a crime where, at the moment, there is none.

***

I stay in Chicago for a week longer than I need to. One full month on Dream Merchants' dime. Or their daily 10K as the case may be.

I figure I deserve it. Hell, thinking about celebs, all the waiting, the damn dirt of seeing into someone else's subconscious, is worth a 300K vacation, even if it is in a hot, sticky urban environment where I know no one.

I do a bit of work, of course. I look at the evidence—sure enough: it's complete, good, accurate, and well-documented. The Chicago Police Department has had a bad reputation for years, but clearly, in this case, they wanted to put the Loop Rapist away forever, and no one made any mistakes.

Then I go back to the basics. I want to make sure that Xavier's path couldn't've crossed Holly Lescoe's and I discover that I'm the one who made a rookie mistake.

Their paths crossed. Their paths crossed major.

They grew up on the same block until Xavier ran away. They went to the same schools, they spent years together in the same rooms.

Maybe he saw her in the Loop that day, maybe he thought of going over to her, talking to her, but was ashamed.

Maybe he saw her with Knickerson, thought she had a boyfriend, and didn't want to bother her.

Or maybe she talked to him, tried to save him like girls of that age were wont to do, and he pushed her away—into the arms of Knickerson.

I have a hunch we'll never know. After all, Knickerson's a rapist and murderer: there ain't no trusting what he says. Holly Lescoe's dead. Her friend is still missing. And the only possible witness, Xavier Calliende, has so much to lose by even mentioning this case that he's probably tried to put the whole thing out of his mind.

Which is probably why it all lurks in his subconscious as a nightmare: one that ends with rivers of blood.

***

When I can finally face returning to Dream Merchants and the hunt for the get, I call Morgana. I'm in the fancy hotel, lying on my bed, imagining her in that cruddy car, in the cold, hitting the dispenser for the even cruddier coffee.

"Hey, dollface, it's Max," I say, donning a persona I'd rather forget. "Remember me?"

"Whatcha got for me?" she asks.

"First, tell me about the films and the modeling," I say.

She pauses. She hasn't expected me to take control of the phone call.

"Lots of pretty boy pictures. Some creepy stuff early on—a bit of Heroin Chic, I think—remember those perfume ads from the turn of the century? All those skinny people glomming onto each other in stick-like fashion?—I got those, but they're not rape imagery or anything. They're just gross."

"Nothing else?" I ask.

"Hey, I did a lot of research, especially for me. I even went back into his first agency's archives—after hours, of course."

"Of course," I say, knowing how it worked. She knows someone everywhere that's important. Her ability to move around a modeling agency after it closed is no surprise at all.

"I couldn't find a damn thing," she says. "So I have hopes for you."

"Well," I say, "it's a bust here too."

"You spent a month on a bust?" she asks.

"Yep," I say. "The girl exists, or did. She was the victim of the Loop Rapist. Remember him?"

"No," Morgana says, sounding bored. "I don't do true crime."

So I go into the whole song and dance, telling her the history of the Rapist, all about the evidence, and all the legwork I did. She's yawning a few times, and then she gets silent.

I think—I hope—she's fallen asleep.

Instead, midway through some explanation of DNA, she interrupts me. "Max?"

"What?" I try not to have relief in my voice. She's gonna tell me to shut up, which I will gladly do.

"Did you use an image scan to find the girl?"

"Yep," I say. "I used the tear-stained frame from Xavier's dream and—"

Too late, I realize Morgana's trapped me. I feel my face flush but I go gamely on, hoping she's dumber than she really is.

"—and used one of those research machines. It turned up a missing person poster. Must've been all over Chicago at the time. That's probably how he knew about her."

"C'mon, Max." Morgana isn't dumb. Dammit to hell. "He saw her, didn't he?"

So I tell her. I tell her everything. I remind her that the guy's blameless, that he won't talk for fear of jeopardizing his career, that if this were a true get, he probably would've sued to have the dream images removed from Ice Cream Dreams site.

She uh-uh and uh-has me, and I'm hoping I'm convincing her. I'm convincing me.

When I pause for breath, she says, "When are you coming back here?"

"Day after tomorrow," I say. "I'm booked on a flight out in the morning."

"Report to the L.A. office," she says. "I'm hearing stuff about Cosimo. He might be staying at the Four Seasons. I have a guy on the inside. If we can get the suite next door, we have a perfect get. Except that I'm going to need my best runner."

Me, on the goddamn bike.

I sigh. "I'll be there," I say, and hang up, feeling uneasy. Feeling like it's not over yet.

***

And of course it's not. By the time I get off the plane in L.A., the story's everywhere—mainstream media has picked it up.

Did Xavier Witness a Murder?

Did America's Greatest Action Hero Wimp Out?

Why Couldn't Xavier Save the Girl He Loved?

Talking heads are on the overhead screens in LAX, speculating on the meaning of the dream. The dream they're showing is the raw footage we got a month ago—and they attribute it to Dream Merchants.

They specifically attribute it to Morgana.

She's on the big screen in front of me, pontificating about guilt dreams, repeating the damn pop psychology I rattled at her.

"Maybe he's making these films because he wishes he had been a hero," she says, sounding every bit as oily Walter Winchell and Barbara Walters and Sanford Cooper.

She looks serious. She *sounds* serious. But I know those eyes—days of waiting in the cold make you really familiar with someone's eyes—and she's gloating. She's got the get of the decade, and she's on her way: the expert on the guilt dream as it applies to celebrity.

Another screen cuts away to Xavier, running from a limo to his house on the Oregon Coast. The camera catches his famous face, and because I, like the rest of America, am intimately familiar with all of his moods from his movies, I know what he's feeling:

Devastated.

His life will never be the same.

Because I sat in a fucking condo with a fake fire burning, looking at his subconscious dealing with something I really don't understand and thought I could have a get. A cop get, but a get all the same.

I stand in front of the giant screen, Morgana still talking, happy with her new-found power, and my stomach twists. We're no different after all. It's just different things that make us hot. She wants fame and the power to destroy. I want justice and the power to make things right.

Only I used my limited powers to help hers.

Mistake. Big mistake.

Her eyes—twenty sizes too large, and flat on the screen—sparkle. I can't go back to Dream Merchants. I can't see this woman ever again.

I turn around and head down the corridor toward ticketing. I'm going back to D.C.

I have a different get, one I didn't expect. Congress is full of people with gray areas in their subconscious. Repressed memories, stuffed-away good-time moments, buried actions-not-taken. Lots of guilt dreams in both Houses—and those guilt dreams are bipartisan.

If I can't convince those people to change the laws now, given the look on Xavier's face, given the wreck Morgana and I have just made of his life, then I'll never get the federal laws to change.

I'll have to travel state to state and find some other way to make this illegal. Ban the dreamcording cameras, ban the sale of other people's dreams, ban the sale of dreams altogether.

I'll figure it out. I'll go head-to-head with the entertainment lobby if I have to.

Because I do have to.

Or no one will ever be able to sleep soundly again.

Going Native

God, could you find a duller way to travel?" asks my leggy companion, the luscious Ruth. She has this weekend off, and she insisted on coming with me on my assignment. It'll be fun, she said, and then followed that up with, how can I know what you're doing unless I come along with you on occasion? I listened to the logic of that, and now I find myself trapped in a 5' by 6' moving room with a woman who finds train travel passé.

Me, I'm afraid that the Amtrak trip up the mountain will be the best part of this assignment. I work for eight online editors, and all of them called me last week to ask for an article on the annual TVS convention. Such a uniformity of requests has only happened once before in my career, and that was when a woman that I sat beside in grade school, tormented in middle school, and dated in high school was inaugurated as president of the United States. Suddenly my memoirs had value.

Somehow, I doubt that this essay has the same sort of import.

I also had my doubts about bringing Ruth to kooksville and now, when we're still two hours away from our destination, I know I've made the Wrong Decision. She is lying on the bottom berth, her bare feet against the dirty plastic wall, her skirt pooled around her waist, and she is not thinking of sex.

Neither am I.

"I mean, we've been on this train for *hours*. How did people travel like this?"

They made love, they ate, they read books. But I do not tell Ruth that. She would see it as a slap, an insult to her great intelligence. In real life, Ruth is a receptionist for a lawyer, but she prefers to call herself a paralegal. She uses legalese, mispronouncing most of it, and pretends that she knows as much as someone who has a law degree.

I've never told her about mine. But then, why should I? It would ruin the sleazy nature of the relationship, the fact that I'm dating her for her deliciously man-made breasts and she's dating me because I know the secrets of the universe.

She believes that's because I'm a journalist. The old-fashioned print kind, even though what we print is done online. I'm paid by the download, which is why I'm on this train trip instead of say, investigating the latest bombing in downtown Seattle. No matter how idealistic you start, you soon learn that it's paranoia that sells.

Which is why we're on a train instead of teleporting. There are no teleportation stations in this part of the Cascades. Rumor has it that the first teleportation technician who ventured into this part of Oregon was shot. Whether he lived or died depends on which rumor you believe.

Ruth knew we were heading into no man's land when she decided to come with me, but the closer we get the less I believe she actually *understood* it. I think she thought we'd look at the crazy yokels and then go home.

I think I thought she could handle anything.

Check that. I think I knew, deep down, she was contemplating Marriage, and I wanted to convince her that breaking up was her idea. But that's hindsight. Going in, I was simply concerned about the lack of sex.

"Once," I say, gazing out the window at the snow beside the tracks, "this was the fastest way to travel in the whole world."

"Yeah." She flops an arm over her eyes, missing the deer that stand by a group of trees, staring at us. A 19th century vision in the 21st. "Sad, isn't it?"

I'm not sure. I'm enough of a romantic to enjoy the view. I'm enough of a romantic to wish that she'd enjoy it with me.

***

The assignment, if you look at it historically (which is one of the few things that I've retained from law school, a sense of historical perspective), is a perennial: Go look at the fringe and report back to the masses. Around the turn of the last century, that meant going to carnivals and fairs to examine the bearded women, the two-headed chickens, and the stillborn fetuses that looked like fish. In my grandfather's day, a reporter on this beat might go to see the mysterious Area 51, thought to be a repository for Unidentified Flying Objects (things so familiar they were known by their acronym UFO) and for the little green men who flew them. Me, I get assigned the annual meeting of the Teleportation Victims Society whose own acronym is TVS, but who is known in newsrooms nationwide as TVSo?. I should've known I was in trouble when I tried to explain this little joke to Ruth and she'd stared at me blankly, not even threatening to smile.

The TVSo?s meet every year in Harbor, Oregon, which used to be a 1990s survivalist camp between Bend and Klamath Falls. The area's only attraction, or so I could glean before I arrived, is that it has no teleportation station, and none is planned. If someone wants to travel in that part of the Cascade Range, they either have to go to Bend, fifty miles to the north, or Klamath Falls, over 60 miles to the south. Then they have to take whatever ground transportation is available, provided, of course, they can get it. Amtrak still serves this part of the country, partly because the sparse population can't justify the teleportation system, and partly because the tracks have existed for nearly two hundred years. It's the only form of public transportation between those two stations, and mostly it's used by the low-income folks who can't afford the cost of speedier travel.

I insisted on taking the train all the way from Seattle, over Ruth's protests, because I wanted my experience at the annual meeting to reflect the experience of all the other TVSo?s. I had secretly hoped I'd meet a few of them on this ride, but Ruth has kept me chained to the room, demanding room service, and not paying for it in the way that I had hoped.

Still I manage to sneak to the club car once, and there I see exactly what I expect, a group of tired, smelly people, most of whom are too drunk to look at the magnificent scenery whizzing past. I realize that, in my new khakis and bomber jacket, I am overdressed and as conspicuous as a rich man in Olympia. No one will talk to me. They barely manage to look at me.

And, for the first time, I worry about how I'll pull this assignment off.

***

I should say at this stage of article research, I always worry about how I'll pull the assignment off. Even though what I write is dictated into my wrist-top, edited on a larger screen at home, and e-mailed directly to my editor, what I do is really not much different from the work, say, Mark Twain did almost two hundred years ago. He ventured out into places unknown and reported back.

Ernest Hemingway did that, so did Ernie Pyle, and Peter Arnett. The great journalists thrived in times of war. When there is no war—or no war America is interested in—we are stuck with perennials. And no journalist ever became famous by risking his life at a TVSo? convention.

I simply want to go in, find a few things that are amusing, see if I can discover the secret behind the victimology, and return to home base with all parts intact. I know that, by Sunday evening, I will have a story. I'm just not sure if it's the kind of story Hemingway would have dispatched from Spain.

In fact, I know it's not the moment the train pulls into Harbor, Oregon.

***

When Ruthie and I get off the train at the small white station nestled against a snow-covered ridge, we are greeted like visiting royalty. I made no secret of my job as a journalist, but it's really Ruthie they want to see. It seems, on the e-slip she sent with her fee, that she listed her employment as she always does.

A paralegal and a journalist. We are a dream couple for the TVSo?s.

I am not the only journalist in this place. Every major television reporter, radio commentator, vid producer, and holotechnician is here to record the loonies in action. I am one of the few print people, and the only one with enough awards to make me semi-famous. Every TVSo? wants to tell me his story, to introduce me to little Jonnie or Suzy or Uncle Billy, and to show me what makes them different.

When I get off the train, I realize I am not ready for this. The grasping hands, the slightly desperate gaze. I insist on going to the hotel before meeting people, and Ruth gives me her I-can't-believe-you're-doing-this look. That's when I realize she's not upset about the location or the people. She's upset that I want to leave them. She not only relishes the attention, she believes she can give these people advice. She doesn't realize how dangerous the situation can be. She's with the only people in the world who might take her seriously. I grip her arm and follow our host to the Compound, our hotel.

The Compound was the former survivalist's camp, and looks it. The outbuildings are made of wood hammered together by people who clearly didn't know what they were doing. The main building, where the restaurant and gift shop reside, was once a ranch-style house, built in the mid-twentieth century, complete with front-facing garage. The building had been added onto, once during its survivalist camp days—that was evident by the concrete bunker in the back—and once by the hotel, the brass and wood façade that tried to make everything upscale.

Our room isn't really a room. It was cabin Number 8. A plaque on the door tells us that it had once been used by the house's original owners as a storage shed, and was remodeled into a cabin when the camp started in the early 1980s. The plaque tells us proudly that eight people lived in this space; I'm wondering how Ruth and I will manage for a weekend.

The room is square, with an area carved out for a bathroom with an ancient shower and plastic tub. The sink has motion detectors instead of computer controls, and the toilet actually has a handle for flushing. Ruth is charmed, but I wonder if that will last into the middle of the night, when one of us stumbles in there and initiates the gurgle and grunt of the ancient plumbing.

We unpack, and then Ruth wants to reenter the fray. I'm more interested in checking out the dining facilities. The reconstituted chicken I had on the train didn't last me long.

Outside, we see several blue-and-white signs, pointing to various cabins. Most signs are hand-lettered and made specifically for the conference: Registration is to our left; Legal advice is to our right; and Testimonials is straight ahead. Other signs show us the way to improve our Education, covering everything from Technological Secrets to the History of Transportation. Many of these, I know, are ongoing programs, and I will check them out through the weekend. It's the guest speakers I am most interested in, and those are going to be the hardest events to see.

***

In the registration line I learn that the TVSo?s aren't all low-income poorly educated folks like the research had led me to expect. The man in front of me is a doctor from Philadelphia who has documentation on "differences" and was willing to call it up on his wrist-top right there in the frigid Oregon mud. The slender, pretty woman behind me is a reasonably well known vid personality whose career went into a decline, she says, after she teleported 65 times in one month. I talk to both of them at some length.

Ruth has left me alone in line while she went on to the lodge for drinks.

She has been gone a long time.

I draw the same sort of crowd I drew at the train station. I am uncomfortable, used to being the observer, not the observed. Everyone wants to tell me a story; everyone wants me to know how teleportation changes people, how it creates differences where there were none before.

Some of the stories are just silly, like the vid personality's. She claims she lost a little bit of charisma each time she teleported from one place to another. Some are strange, like the woman who has me examine holograms of her now-estranged husband, a man whose eye color changed in the space of one afternoon from green to brown.

The rest are merely sad. Many are from people who claim that their spouses are no longer the same people they married, and they blame use of public teleportation. Others show evidence of medical conditions they claim were caused by teleporting, and still some have tales of close loved ones who died soon after traveling in a teleportation device.

I have read the literature; I am familiar with all variations on these stories and more. I even know their origins.

I ask the eye color woman why she believes her husband's eyes were the only thing to change.

"I didn't say they were the only thing, now did I?" she says angrily.

I turn away, afraid to follow up.

***

The first big breakthrough in teleportation occurred in the late 1990s when a team of Austrian scientists successfully completed a transfer on the sub-atomic level. The physics of the breakthrough was too complex to explain to the layman in the popular newspapers of the day, so many journalists attempted [unsuccessfully] to put the discovery in layman's terms.

I have tried to hunt down the origin of the example used for the laymen and have been, to date, unsuccessful. I suspect either one of the scientists got exasperated with the journalists' stupid questions and used the example to explain, poorly, what was going on, or a journalist attempted to translate what he thought he understood into language that he thought other people could understand.

Their experiment, said the news organizations of the day, was as if the scientists had taken a red ball in one room, made it disappear, and then reappear in another room—although what was teleported was not the ball itself, but the *quality* of redness which was then transferred onto another ball.

It is not what we experience. We experience the teleportation first imagined in pulp fiction stories of over a hundred years ago. Our bodies literally disassemble in one location, are transferred to another location, and are then reassembled. There are documented cases of malfunctions, most dating from the early days of the technology and almost all of them having to do with apes who arrived dead.

These deaths were not pretty or simple: they had to do with parts being reassembled in the wrong order, rather like taking a puzzle apart, then trying to put it together by placing all the corners in the middle. Those details were resolved long before any human being stepped onto a teleportation pad. The things we must worry about are simpler: power failures and computer malfunctions, both of which can lose us mid-transfer. This problem is the greatest in Third World countries, in devices built out of scrap metal, most likely, by the operator's Uncle Ralph. Teleportation is not sanctioned to those countries, or is done purely at the user's own risk. Here and in "approved" countries, every device is scrutinized, overhauled, and replaced more often than anything else in our technologically advanced society.

This is what the literature tells me. It is what exists in all published reports, the meetings before Congress, and in several teleportation companies' legal databases. I know there can be problems—we all do. The problems are called "acceptable risk," something we all assume when we step on a teleportation pad, or even when we walk out our front door. What varies from person to person is how acceptable some risks are.

It is the idea that we can be disassembled and reassembled that unnerves people the most. A large number of people (actual estimates vary, depending on the reporting agency) refuse to use teleportation, allowing other forms of mass transit to remain in business. Most of these people are not TVSo?s. They simply don't like the idea of being taken apart and put back together without it being necessary, and are not willing to sacrifice their original unity for the sake of instantaneous travel.

Others cannot imagine traveling any other way. Frequent teleporters receive a discount on each trip. "Frequent" is defined in the industry as anyone making more than ten trips per day. I have only hit the ten trip in one day milestone once, and it left me feeling disoriented and unnerved—not, I hasten to add, because I was disassembled so many times, but because, after five different teleportation stations, I lost track of my surroundings. Later I learned that frequent travelers set their wrist-top to remind them of their location and their purpose for being there upon arrival.

I have read all the literature, examined all the records, and while I still feel a twinge of nerves when I step on the platform, I prefer the instantaneous shift, the delight at having been in Manhattan one moment and Rome the next. It is not different, my grandmother once told me, than that frisson of fear she used to feel whenever an airplane's wheels left the ground or whenever a train went over a particularly high and narrow bridge.

It is human nature to worry about the accidental, the unexpected, the unknown. It is also human nature to magnify those things into problems so strange as to be somehow plausible.

***

The TVSo?s have three banquets at their weekend meeting, and I have bought tickets to all three. Ruth did not want to eat at the banquets. In fact, she soon made it clear that she did not want to spend time with me. She says my attitude is too cynical, my remarks too cutting. She is already right. I am already thinking in the tone I've decided to take for this article, a tone that my brain established while part of it tried to concentrate on the seriousness of the vid personality's loss of charisma.

The first banquet is on Friday night, and there I am happily surprised. The food is excellent. It is free-range chicken, brought in from a nearby ranch, local vegetables grown and stored here, marinated in local wine, mixed with spices grown in the chef's own herb garden.

Nothing was shipped in: no risk of teleportation tainting the food. And somehow it does seem fresher. Or perhaps the chef, a world-renowned man who refused to allow me to use his name in this article, has simply lived up to his spectacular reputation.

The speaker that night is a transportation historian who is, believe it or not, duller than he sounds. He reads his speech off the TelePrompTer modification in his contact lenses, probably much as he does in class, which forces him to stare straight ahead. That, combined with his monotone, makes him seem as if he's teleported one too many times.

The diners at my table, which is toward the back, immediately deduce the problem and begin whispering, as I imagine his students often do. We introduce ourselves and tell each other why we're here.

The woman to my immediate left looks like a Hollywood grandmother, which is to say that she's round, gray-haired and jolly. She confides that she went to see her grandchildren on her only teleportation trip, and instead of arriving in Pittsburgh as planned, she arrived in Philadelphia. The teleportation operators claim she simply told them she was going to Philly, but she claims that they punched in the wrong destination. I take mental notes, knowing that what is at stake here is more than a simple trip. She lives on a fixed income and she scrimped to afford the teleport. She could not afford to then go from Philly to Pittsburgh and back home. She missed a trip, and probably several meals, for that one abortive visit.

This is a problem I can get behind. It is not magic woo-woo incantations in which she claims that she suddenly ballooned in size because her protons expanded or that she got skin cancer that should have belonged to someone else. This is the kind of operator error we all worry about. I have had nightmares about getting on a teleporter in Portland and ending up in Beijing.

The woman next to her confides that there is a lawyer in the legal section who is trying to get enough contacts to initiate a class action suit for just that sort of problem. The grandmother thanks her, and then asks her, whispering politely of course, why she's here. The woman, who is in her mid-forties, has the prettiest lavender hair I've ever seen. She flushes a nice shade of pink that somehow complements the lavender and admits that she would rather not say.

I am beginning to think I've hit a lucky table. Imagine someone who has come to a TVSo? convention who is unwilling to admit why she has come. It is almost antithetical to the purpose of the conference.

I make a mental note to pull her aside later, then ask the man to my right why he has come. "Reporter," he says tersely, not whispering. "Just like you."

He gets shushed by the people at the table behind him, who, believe it or not, are engrossed in the teacher's speech. At that point, I surface briefly, realize the man has droned on for thirty minutes and hasn't yet reached the invention of the automobile. I signal a waiter for more coffee.

The woman to the reporter's right bursts into tears when asked why she's here, and we get shushed again. I actually don't mind because I get an odd sense that the tears are fake. Still, we dutifully lean forward after she dries her eyes with her linen napkin.

"My baby," she whispers, and stifles a sob. The entire table behind us glares at us with angry eyes. We glare back, then lean as close as we can.

"My baby," she says again, "was a boy when he went into the device."

Suddenly I don't want to hear any more, and neither, it seems, does anyone else. The reporter hands her another napkin, and makes sympathetic noises, but as quickly as he politely can, he rises and makes his way to the men's room.

Ten minutes later, when he has not returned and the speaker is rhapsodizing about the uses of airplanes in World War I, I excuse myself. The corridor outside is empty, but I find a new convention going on at the bar.

"I don't know why they invite him back," says one woman to a gale of laughter. It seems that this is the fifth year the historian has spoken on Friday night, and this year he is actually *more* interesting than he has ever been.

One of the conference organizers overhears, and says rather stiffly, "We invite him so that you all have an historical overview of the problems we face."

"Oh," the laughing woman says, "but don't you think that teleportation is a little different than, say, a Model T?"

"No," the organizer says, and I realize that this is one of those dangerous people to whom the phrase "sense of humor" has no meaning at all, "it is all a manifestation of our need to make the world smaller. Once everyone thought that instantaneous travel would solve all our ills. They didn't realize that it would cause more problems than it started."

"Do you believe," one woman asks, "that everyone who has been in a teleportation device is still human?"

Not even the conference organizer answers that question. It is too touchy. Most of the people here are here because they have been in a teleportation device. If the woman's right, that would mean none of us are human. I don't believe that. I believe we're very human, although the more I see, the more I wonder what side of humanity we actually belong to.

***

The next morning, I wander over to Legal, and listen to lawyers pontificate on ways to collect damages from teleportation companies. I hear the familiar litany of successful lawsuits—there aren't many, and most are nuisance cases much like the grandmother's of the night before—but the audience is attentive and asks polite questions.

In the afternoon, I poke my head into Education, and see the historian. I don't run from there, although I'm tempted. I walk slowly, pretending I had ventured into that area by mistake.

Ruth is nowhere to be seen. She did show up in our room the night before, but long after I was asleep, and I thought I smelled brandy, but by that point I didn't really care. I wonder idly who she has found to entertain herself with and how she can use him to further her career. The thought, though accurate, is uncharitable, and I then wonder when I stopped thinking with fondness of Ruth's tendency's to exaggerate and began to be annoyed by them. Probably around the point when her manufactured breasts became her most fascinating feature.

That night's speaker is an expert in teleportation technology and I am assured by almost everyone who's been here before that he makes the historian look glib. I am sorry to give up the free-range chicken, but I cannot bear another two hours trapped in those uncomfortable wooden banquet chairs.

I go into the restaurant, where I've had two delicious breakfasts, and cast about for a table. It seems to have a lot of patrons, considering there is a banquet going on in the next room.

Ruth is at a table near the window. Even though it is dark, I can make out the ghostly shape of the nearby mountain, snow-covered and shiny. She waves me over.

She is sitting with the lawyers. They have asked that no other tables be filled around them, and so far the restaurant is able to comply. Ruth, it seems, has been spending her time with the entire legal wing of this conference and learning "a whole heckuva lot."

I sit down, and listen for a while. This seems like an informal version of the panel I had attended in the morning. I order a steak, and do not ask if it was shipped in or slaughtered locally, for which I am razzed, and then one of the attorneys, an overweight vegetarian who consumes way too much wine during the evening, informs me of the many ways that beef could kill me. Since I have heard this lecture before, I add a few insights of my own, all the while chomping heartily on my dinner.

Finally they ask me why I'm here, and I tell them that I'm a paid observer of human nature.

"He's journalist," Ruth says, breaking my cover.

They eye me as if *I'm* the slimy species and I explain that I'm a practitioner of New Journalism almost a century after New Journalism was introduced. It is my way of gaining legitimacy among the illegitimate: pretend to a literary value that I don't really have.

The New Journalism comment seems to have silenced them, so to break the ice—and to make my dinner worthwhile—I ask them what they really think about teleportation technology.

"It makes lawyers rich!" one of them said and the others laugh. But I press them, and finally a dark-suited man next to Ruth says, "I used to laugh at these folks and then questions started coming up, questions I couldn't get an answer to."

One of the female attorneys nods, and still another, the overweight vegetarian, says, "Yeah, like why is there a ban on kids under the age of three taking teleportation?"

"It's not a firm ban," a New York lawyer says. "You can get around it with a doctor's permission."

"Yeah," the vegetarian says. "Why a doctor? And what does he give permission for?"

"I've never seen any instances of babies traveling. They don't allow it, with or without the doctor," the woman says.

"But I met a woman who says her baby—" I start and they all shake their heads sadly, silencing me.

"She's here every year," the vegetarian says. "I checked the story out. She doesn't have a kid. I don't even think she's female."

They chuckle again, and the joviality is back. No matter how I push them, I can't learn what the other questions are. The vegetarian promises to tell me if I come to the bar later. I do, and he's passed out in a pile of corn chips. I vow to try and find him the following day.

***

The next morning, as the speakers are setting up, I go to the Technological Secrets area. It's in a wide auditorium with holographic capabilities. My mind boggles just at the thought of seeing strange machinery in life-size and 3D.

It takes me a moment to find a speaker who'll talk to me, who doesn't try to get me to wait until his presentation. I tell him about the lawyers' collective unease about the baby ban.

"You ask the teleportation stations they'll tell you it's because babies are too fragile for most kinds of travel. Like they'll ban an infant from a jet." The guy I'm talking to is six feet tall and has a honking nasal voice. I'm glad I elected not to stay for his presentation, even though he seems nice enough. "But it's really because of the stress to the body."

"I thought there is no stress."

He looks at me as if I'm the dumbest thing he's seen at this conference, and given what I've seen, I'm almost insulted. He holds up a glass of water. "You can't teleport crystal either," he says. "Sometimes it shatters. And it shouldn't. I mean, they perfected this at the subatomic level, or so they say."

"You don't think they did?"

"Between you, me, and the wall," he says, "I know they perfected it. The problem is that they don't use the right equipment to teleport people. It's like building a house. We can build a damn fine house with everything correct. But we hire contractors who want to make as much money as possible, and they do it—have done it—since time immemorial by using inferior parts and charging the same as they would for good parts. I try to tell the lawyers that, but it's not glamorous, and it's damned hard to prove. They tell me they'll help me when I can show damage caused by inferior parts. I can show damage. I just can't make a credible link."

Later that day, I check his statements with a few other technology wonks. They agree that the problem with public teleportation is that it's *public.* The system used by the President and other heads of state is state-of-the-art, so protected that nothing can go wrong. The system used by the rest of us, well, these guys would have us all believe it's held together by spit and glue and pieces manufactured just after the turn of the century.

It makes me think of all those bans on teleportation travel to third-world countries. If our technology is bad, what is the technology like that was hammered together by someone's Uncle Ralph? The very idea raises images of those poor puzzle box monkeys with the corners where their middle should be.

Of course when I get back home, and call the various teleportation manufacturers, they all give me the company line and swear teleportation is the safest form of transportation since walking. Even that can go wrong, I say. Think of potholes. Think of missteps, twisted ankles and tripping over small children. But the manufacturers don't find me funny. When I get belligerent, forgetting, for a moment that this is supposed to be a puff piece and not investigative reporting, they transfer me to their legal departments who remind me of libel laws and how careful I need to be in questioning their companies.

***

The free-range chicken is gone by the third banquet, but the speaker is delightful. He's a comedian just starting out, and he proves to me that the TVSo?s have a sense of humor, since most of his jokes are aimed at them, and they laugh uproariously. I don't. I feel vaguely embarrassed, mostly because I know I would have laughed if I'd been watching this guy in any other setting but this one.

As I head out, I look for Ruth. She's still surrounded by her lawyers, and when she sees me, she waves me over. She puts a hand on the overweight vegetarian's arm and informs me that he has hired her as a paralegal. I pull her aside, remind her that jobs aren't always that easy to come by and that she'd better check his credentials. She frowns at me, asks me if I think she's dumb or something—a question which I decline to answer—and then stalks off. I gather, from that whole exchange, that she's not taking the train home, and I turn out to be right. My wish has been granted. She has forgotten thoughts of Marriage and believes that our break-up is her idea. I find that I regret the whole plan, not because I wanted to marry her, but because I had hoped that I would at least get to try all parts of train travel, from meal to sleep to sex. We had neglected sex on the way there, and I was hoping for a bit on the way home.

Instead, I spend the next week finding a way to ship her clothes cheaply without using teleportation technology, since the vegetarian likes to keep his office "pure."

I am beginning to understand the sentiment. My moment of hesitation as I step on the teleportation platform in Bend—I see no point in train travel all the way to Seattle if I'm not going to be able to have nookie in transit—lasts nearly three minutes, and customers behind me get angry. But I keep thinking of those banned babies, and Uncle Ralph, and inferior-grade equipment, and the way that the sheet rock in my condo flakes like someone's untended dandruff, and I find myself more and more reluctant to travel in that instantaneous sort of way. After all, why am I in such a hurry? I'm a journalist, for godssake, a man who makes his living off observing, and observation is something that can't be rushed. I am proud of my observation skills, and proud of my capability for contemplation that makes them possible.

But what I've been observing since I got back is my own reflection in the mirror. There's a line down one side of my face, an instant wrinkle that really doesn't look like a laugh line or something that would naturally occur as I age. It looks more like a fold, or a crease, something incorrectly ironed in, as if a section of me were miscut and hemmed wrong.

I never noticed the wrinkle before getting on that teleportation station in Bend. I have been obsessed with it since. And I think, I really think, that my obsession is a product of the TVSo? convention, but not for the reason that you'd think. It's not that I suddenly believe the teleporter has given me a new wrinkle. It's just that I find the idea of a wrinkle induced from the outside better than the idea that I'm growing older. It's easier to believe in the fiction. It's nicer.

It takes the responsibility for that particular line off me.

Or at least, that's what I tell myself. Because I do need to teleport on occasion for my job. Journalists observe, yes. But they must observe in the right places. And when my editor tells me to get to London yesterday, I do the next best thing. I get there two minutes from now, new wrinkles be damned.

But I find that I do examine mirrors more, and I wonder, when I think something particularly cruel, like most of my thoughts about Ruth lately, if I've become less than human. Is humanity something we can lose, little bit by little bit, like the vid personality and her charisma? And if so, how can we tell it's gone? Is it replaced by paranoia, by worry, in equal degrees? And am I, in worrying about this, showing signs of latent TVSo?ism?

I don't know. But I do suspect that my recent desire to take the train to the far reaches of the United States has less to do with my unfulfilled sexual fantasy than it does with my desire to avoid a technology that I may have learned to fear. Then I remind myself of the history of this form of paranoia; I know that being a reporter from the fringe requires an ability to cross over into that land and appear to be a native. I'm simply afraid I've taken it too far. Going native requires residency in kooksville, and while it only takes an instant to reach that particular destination, it takes years and expensive psychotherapy to get out.

***

When I turned in this essay, I thought of asking for a bonus, a sort of combat pay to compensate for the wrinkle, for the increased harassment as I take an extra minute of other people's time while I hesitate before stepping on a teleportation platform.

But my editor vid-conferenced with me this morning, wanting to discuss what he calls "proper compensation." My article, he says—(this thing you are currently reading, without this coda)—has given him an idea. Teleportation has overtaken other forms of transportation so much that his younger readers have probably never flown in a plane or driven a car. He wants me to do these things, and report back about my experiences, as if I have gone to yet another frontier, even if it is a part of the past.

He asks what I want to do first, and then reminds me this will be on the magazine's expense.

"A ticket on the Orient Express," I say.

"Ah," he says. "You'll title it 'Strangers on a Train?'"

I'm thinking not of Patricia Highsmith and Alfred Hitchcock, but of luscious, willing blonds with breasts the size of helium balloons and the ca-thunk, ca-thunk of the wheels on a track suggesting a rhythm that no teleportation device can hope to match.

"I hope so," I say, and realize this is the kind of fringe I like. "I certainly hope so."

What Fluffy Knew

Fluffy knew she was a princess. Her person told her so. And Fluffy herself could see it, in her white, white fur, her long elegant whiskers, and her dainty paws. Fluffy had a soft bed that smelled of cedar. She had as much food as she wanted. People came to her house, and when she presented herself, they all spoke in awe of her beauty and petted her gingerly, as if they couldn't believe they were allowed to touch her sacred body. She bumped them gently to let them know that petting was preferred in her kingdom, and they usually responded with a laugh and a good ear rub.

Life was good. It didn't even matter that her people occasionally took in other cats. There had been other cats in her life as long as she was alive. She knew, however, that they weren't as great as she was. No other cat was as beautiful or as soft or as well loved. Other cats lived with her, and she tolerated them. She would have put up a large fuss, but her people had found a new palace, one with many rooms, and she rarely saw the other cats, except at feeding times.

Her routine was perfect in its simplicity. She spent her mornings in the kitchen waiting for someone to brush her, her afternoons sprawled on the couch in the warm sunshine, and her evenings on the nearest lap. Sometimes she watched the water droplets in the bathtub after her people took showers.

Nights were her special time. She prowled and explored, took food her people sometimes left near the sink, and occasionally slept on their soft bed. She was in her cedar bed at dawn just to make sure no one else used it, and then she was up, beginning her routine all over again.

Yes. It was a very good life.

Until *they* came.

***

"Please give the boys a thorough examination. I'll pay you extra. I know your time is limited when you do your house calls, and I appreciate the fact that so few vets do such a thing, but this has me bothered."

"Mrs. Winters, what's happened is tragic, but not uncommon. These adorable creatures are miniature lions. We think they're civilized, but they're not. And occasionally they remind us, often in particularly unpleasant ways."

***

They seemed to know who the weak ones were. Later, Fluffy found herself wondering: if she had known what *they* were going to do, would she have crushed *them* on that first day? Would she have stopped *them*? *They* were, after all, little bigger than a flea. But even fleas were hard to kill, weren't they? She had had fleas as a kitten, before she was elevated to her proper position, and she remembered the sudden sharp pain of the bite, the uncontrollable urge to scratch, the impossibility of catching a flea between your teeth. So perhaps she wouldn't have been able to do anything even if she had been paying attention. Even if she tried to stop the problem on the day it had started.

They went for her littermate, Streaker, and his little friend, Rook. Streaker's royal blood was diluted by his street-tough father, a swaggering Tom that Fluffy barely remembered from her kittenhood. Her own father was a sweet white cat, a little on the fat side, just as her mother was. A "Pedigreed Pair," her former people used to say. The litter, they said to the people who would become her people, was ruined by the black-and-white kitten. A Tom had gotten to their precious girl at the right time. So they had to give the kittens away, unable to prove the purity of their bloodline.

Her people didn't care. They liked the black-and-white kitten with the impish streak, and they named him Streaker because he liked to run from one end of the house to the other for no apparent reason. He refused to show her the proper respect, slapping at her when she got in his way, or demanding that she give up her food. His little friend Rook, a long-haired tabby, showed many of the same behaviors. Rook was a stray her people had rescued, and to them he was kind. To her, he was as insensitive as her brother.

But she could avoid them—and often did. Streak and Rook spent most of their time together, sleeping, eating, playing. She spent most of her time with her human companions, as it should be.

So the afternoon *they* appeared, she thought nothing of it.

***

"Yes, but they've never done anything like this before. I'm beginning to wonder if something's wrong—"

"Trust me, Mrs. Winters. We get complaints like this all the time when housecats show their animal natures. There's nothing wrong."

***

It was summer. Her favorite window was open, the one overlooking the garden and the birds. She could smell flowers, which sometimes made her sneeze; other cats, which always made her curious; and birds, which usually made her want to be slightly energetic, in a wholly disgusting way. She, as her people always told her, was a princess, and didn't have to kill her own food. The boys, as her people called Streaker and Rook, didn't quite understand that, but the other two cats, Starlight and Cupcake, did. They preferred to sleep and eat, just as she did, and fortunately for her, weren't as good at attracting pets.

She had been asleep in the sun below her favorite window when *they* arrived. Rook and Streaker were sprawled in the door, playing their nasty little game: Trap Fluffy. If she hissed at them, they would jump on her and pull at her fur. If she pretended not to notice, they would leave her alone and eventually grow tired of the game. She had decided not to notice, and the hot sun had put her to sleep.

A slight whirring sound woke her up. She sat up, stretched and saw a tiny machine, rather like the ones her people watched on the box in the living room, a round machine that had doors and windows too tiny for any cat to use.

The fur rose on the back of her neck and she felt a hiss start in the back of her throat. But something warned her not to hiss. She didn't want to call attention to herself. Instead, she slipped beneath the couch, and watched.

The little door opened, and tiny human shaped creatures emerged. They were no bigger than ants. They spoke a strange language, stranger than the one her people used. It was much harder to understand. The creatures had other creatures held by silver threads—leashes as thin as spider webs and nearly as invisible. Fluffy watched as the bigger creatures unhooked the leashes, snapped their fingers, and pointed toward the door.

The smaller creatures flew across the room, like tiny flies on a mission. The larger creatures went back through the door. Fluffy heard a whirring sound, and the tiny machine was gone.

She adjusted her position under the couch, and saw the small creatures fly into Rook's left ear. Another group of them flew into Streaker's right ear.

And then the terror began.

***

"What about the alien virus?"

"Mrs. Winters—"

"Don't use that tone with me, Doctor. I've been doing some reading—"

"Tabloids."

"They mentioned it on CNN. They said that ever since those tiny spaceships landed—"

"There's no proof that those are spaceships, Mrs. Winters."

"—animals have been acting strangely. You told me yourself last month, when you gave Cupcake her shots that all sorts of strange things were happening to the animals in town."

"I was talking about illnesses."

"Well, so am I. Rook and Streaker haven't been acting normally, and I'm really worried about the other cats..."

***

Rook let out a yelp like a cat in severe pain, and Streaker shook his head as if something were biting him. Then they ran in opposite directions, and Fluffy didn't see them for the rest of the day.

Of course, she had to go back to sleep. The spot under the couch, despite the dirt, was much more comfortable than she had expected.

She didn't see the attack on the dog.

It was, or so her people said later in very excited tones, extremely strange. Their neighbor had brought his dog over when he came to get a package one of her admirers—the one who drove the loud brown truck—had left. Rook and Streaker bit the dog's legs and made him bleed before her people could pull them off. Her people apologized, but the neighbor got upset. Fluffy never did understand that part. It was just a dog, after all. She was more concerned about the smelly blood all over the kitchen floor.

Rook and Streaker licked it up, and smacked their lips as if they'd had a particularly tasty treat. Her male person had said it was fortunate the boys were up to date on their shots or the entire experience would have been a costly one.

The other cats chalked it up to Dog Phobia, but Fluffy didn't. She saw the look in their eyes. She had been their target many times, and she had never seen them look so sad after an attack. Usually they were gleeful. Instead, they smacked their lips and scratched their ears, and when they finally fell asleep, they whined.

A lot.

She made sure they were nowhere near her as she prowled and snacked later that night.

***

"One article, in the local paper, said a university researcher thought that the aliens were experimenting on mammals as test cases before they started experimenting on humans."

"Mrs. Winters, really."

"I know it sounds silly, but after what the boys did, I'm looking for any explanation. Please, Doctor. Take just a few moments. Examine them."

***

For the first three days, they tried to get outside, but her people were too fast for them. The boys were getting older and were well fed and didn't move as fast as they used to. Their people stopped them at the door, every time, usually with a foot blocking their way. And then they turned their attention on the other cats.

Cupcake, the obese Persian who wanted Fluffy's spot as princess of the house, found a hiding spot behind the dryer. Fluffy stayed close to her people because she knew the boys wouldn't attack her in public. But Starlight, the black and gold stray, wasn't so lucky.

The boys cornered Starlight behind the toilet, and had ripped out her throat before their people could stop it. Their male person took the boys and threw them in cat carriers. Their female person tried to save Starlight. She bundled her in a towel and took her to the Emergency Vet, a place Fluffy had—fortunately—never seen.

The boys spent the night in cages in the garage. Their people promised a Mobile Vet visit in the morning. Cupcake slept well for the first time in a week.

Fluffy woke once and shivered. The boys were wailing as if they had seen the end of the world.

***

"All right, Mrs. Winters. I'll examine them. But before I do, let me be blunt. Starlight was a very old, malnourished stray. She wasn't part of your cat family."

"Yes, she was."

"Not to the cats. And it might not have mattered even if they had known her well. Cats live in prides and have hierarchies. And one rule that exists from lions to barn cats is that the alpha male destroys the weak so that the rest have enough to eat."

"They have enough to eat."

"It doesn't matter. It's in the genetic code."

"We've taken in strays before and they've never—you know. Killed the cat."

"Maybe the other strays weren't as sick."

"You don't think you'll find anything, do you?"

"No."

***

Fluffy hated puzzles, and she really didn't like the boys. They harassed her and didn't give her the respect that royalty deserved. But she didn't like to hear anyone cry either. And her person was right: they hadn't killed Starlight. Those creatures inside them had.

She had to get those creatures out of the boys. And she had to do it without infecting herself or Cupcake.

The creatures had gone in the ear. The Mobile Vet had cold wet stuff that went in the ear. She had seen him use it on Starlight just last week. Maybe that would be enough to get the creatures out.

But how to tell her person and the Mobile Vet what she knew? They would think, if she wound around their legs, that she wanted pets. And even though they thought themselves superior, they never had mastered Fluffy's language, not like she had mastered theirs. The problem was she couldn't speak it; she hadn't seen the use for it until now.

Her person had brought Streaker in from the garage. He had dried blood on his muzzle and his eyes were wide and dark. He looked like a cat in pain to Fluffy.

Her person put Streaker's cat carrier on the kitchen counter, and started to open the gate. Fluffy had to act now. She took a flying leap—something she hadn't done since she was a kitten—and landed on the Vet's medical bag.

He made a small sound and her person spoke her name in that sharp reprimanding tone. Fluffy ignored her. Instead she scratched on the top of the bag until a corner of it pulled back. She put a paw under it, and clung as the vet tried to lift her off.

Instead, he helped her open the bag.

There were rows of needles inside, and lots of little vials. She tried not to watch when he worked on the other cats, and she could barely remember what he had done to Starlight's ear.

He hadn't used a needle. He had used a bottle. A small white bottle that liquid dripped out of.

She only had a moment. She batted a bottle aside, and it rolled along the floor. Then she wriggled out of the vet's grasp and jumped on the counter.

Her person reprimanded her again. Fluffy stopped in front of Streaker's cage and scratched her ear. He frowned at her. She scratched her other ear, and her person shoved her on the floor.

She landed with an unceremonious thump, and she had to pause to lick herself. No princess ever allowed herself to be shoved like that, not even in the name of justice.

From above, she heard the sound of a back foot thumping against a plastic cage.

Streaker had understood.

***

"They're too big to be ear mites."

"Then what are they?"

"I don't know. But I'm going to take them to the lab with me and investigate. I'll leave this vial with you. If you see any more of them, scoop them up and bring them to me. Don't let them near the cats."

"Should we do the other cats?"

"Probably. Yes. Get them. We'd best make sure this is taken care of. Something this big in your ear would be painful. We don't want it to happen again."

***

For her troubles, she was grabbed, held by the scruff of the neck, and had cold liquid shoved down her ear, with instructions to have the same procedure repeated until the liquid was gone. Both the vet and her person were pleased to see that no creatures came out of her ears.

And then they went off to find Cupcake.

Streaker looked at her from his cage. She looked back. His eyes closed slowly. She had never seen a cat seem so exhausted—and so relieved.

***

"Doctor?"

"Mmm?"

"Are those bugs what made my boys kill Starlight?"

"I can't answer that for sure, Mrs. Winters. I don't know what these bugs are or what they do."

"But the boys, will they hurt my other cats?"

"Cats aren't like dogs, Mrs. Winters. Once dogs get a taste for blood, they usually must be kept outside or destroyed. Cats—the thing that your cats did—is natural. They hurt things one minute and cuddle with their owner the next. Will your cats be the same loving creatures you've always known?

Of course. Will they hurt Cupcake and Fluffy? Not unless they get so sick that they're a threat to the pride. I would say that you separate your cats in the future when one of them gets ill. That'll ensure something like this will never happen again."

"So I can let them have the run of the house, and they won't hurt anyone again?"

"If you follow my instructions."

"I will. Oh, Doctor. How will I ever forgive them for Starlight?"

"Realize they're not human, and that human laws don't apply. What they did was right in the feline world."

"That doesn't work for me."

"Then blame it on the bugs."

***

Three days later, Fluffy was asleep in the sun beneath her favorite window. The boys were cuddled on the couch, still exhausted from their ordeal.

A whir woke Fluffy up. She rolled over and saw the tiny machine on the windowsill. The little door opened and the bigger creatures came out. They held tiny whistles in their hands.

The high-pitched sound woke up the boys. They glanced at Fluffy. She glanced at them. Then she reached up with one paw, and knocked the machines—and the bigger creatures—off the sill.

The boys jumped down beside her, and the hunt began.

It was Rook who discovered that if you bit one of the creatures halfway between its head and its feet and then threw it against the wall, it didn't move again. Streaker discovered that a paw through the door crushed the little machines.

But Fluffy was the one who figured out how to knock down machines mid-flight; Fluffy who figured out how to dodge the tiny rays of light that hurt more than a needle's prick; Fluffy who figured out how to flush the machines down the toilet so that they would be gone for good.

Because Fluffy knew if the creatures and their tiny machines succeeded in taking over Rook and Streaker, they might take over her. And if they took over her, and discovered how wonderful her life was, it wouldn't be long before they sent for more little machines and sent bugs into the ears of her people. And once they had control of her people, they had control of the entire world.

And Fluffy couldn't let that happen. In this world, she was a princess. And she would remain a princess—even if it meant dirtying her paws to do so.

The creatures hadn't known what they were up against.

But Fluffy knew.

And Fluffy won.

Just like she knew she would.

About the Author

International bestselling writer Kristine Kathryn Rusch has won two Hugo awards, a World Fantasy Award, and six Asimov's Readers Choice Awards. Her latest sf novel is *Blowback: A Retrieval Artist Novel* from WMG Publishing. The next novel in her acclaimed Diving Universe, *Skirmishes*, will be published by WMG Publishing in September 2013. For her less serious work, check out her Kristine Grayson paranormal romance novels. For more information about her writing, please go to kristinekathrynrusch.com.

Also by
Kristine Kathryn Rusch

The Retrieval Artist Series:

The Disappeared
Extremes
Consequences
Buried Deep
Paloma
Recovery Man
Duplicate Effort
Anniversary Day
Blowback

The Diving Series (novellas):

Diving into the Wreck
The Room of Lost Souls
Becalmed
Becoming One with the Ghosts
Stealth
Strangers at the Room of Lost Souls
The Spires of Denon

www.ingramcontent.com/pod-product-compliance
Lightning Source LLC
LaVergne TN
LVHW091003080826
845145LV00003B/1109

* 9 7 8 0 6 1 5 8 0 9 7 6 2 *